## Advance Praise for
## *My Name Is Cinnamon*

'In *My Name Is Cinnamon*, Vikas Joshi brings to life the lively tale of Cinnamon, a young boy living with his adoptive parents, who sets out to meet his birth parents in an impoverished tribal area. This emotionally sensitive topic is explored with felicity and humour, reminding us of the immense joys and painful travails of childhood. It's a moving and uplifting book, and I wish Vikas Prakash Joshi all the best for his future writing success.'

—Dr Shashi Tharoor
Politician, writer, and former international diplomat

'A richly textured narrative of a "heart-baby" born of a mixed marriage who grows up and goes in search of his roots. An interesting and uplifting read in a time of social schisms.'

—Jug Suraiya
Author, journalist, and former associate editor, *The Times of India*

'With gentle humour and empathy, Vikas Prakash Joshi has taken on the rites of passage of an adopted child. A book to be read by adults and children in order to broaden horizons.'

—Paro Anand
Author, Bal Sahitya Puraskar winner, and former head, National Centre for Children's Literature and National Book Trust

'Cinnamon is a heart-warming story that is bound to make you smile and tear up, and it will definitely suck you into its innocent world, which will make you reminisce about your own childhood and smile once again.'

—Anirban Bhattacharya
Bestselling author, producer, actor, stand-up comedian, and public speaker

'*My Name Is Cinnamon* is a fun journey, delivered with astute observations, witty humour, and life lessons. I am sure children will love it.'

—Dr Manjiri Prabhu
Bestselling author, screenplay writer, and founder-director, Pune International Literary Festival

'It evokes Pune with its vada pav, football matches, Shrewsbury biscuits, and mist-shrouded winter mornings.'

—Dr Easterine Kire, Norway
Winner of the Bal Sahitya Puraskar, Tata Literature Live! prize, and Hindu Literature prize

'*My Name Is Cinnamon* is Vikas Joshi's promising debut novella. Vikas has managed to address a very sensitive issue with a lot of humour, irony, and understanding which makes the book a useful tool for

*contd . . .*

families of adopted children and professionals working in these areas without taking away the enjoyable reading experience for the general audience.'

—Irina Papancheva, Bulgaria
Award-winning author and head of EU advocacy and campaigns, Lumos Foundation

'*My Name Is Cinnamon* is a deeply engrossing read, a highly moving story of adoption, set in a real India and told with brilliance and kindly humour.'

—Ashok Rajagopalan
Acclaimed author, illustrator, and former art editor, Tulika Publications

'It is a real pleasure to read a story set in a world so culturally different from my own, yet so recognisable in its underlying emotions. It's proof that we are all part of the same world family, even if we are continents apart.'

—Mandy Hager, New Zealand
Bestselling author, recipient of Margaret Mahy Medal, and president, New Zealand Society of Authors

'*My Name Is Cinnamon* is heartwarming, like a rice pudding sprinkled with cinnamon, a deeply touching story to savour and remember.'

—Aylin Oney Tan, Turkey
Columnist, *Hurriyet Daily News* and *Cumhuriyet*

'In the present society, where self-interest and solitude are highly promoted, Vikas portrays a new avenue enriched with humour, adventure, and wonder, displaying the talent of an experienced painter.'

—Chulananda Samaranayake, Sri Lanka
Award-winning poet, and head of translators pool,
Ministry of Public Administration, Provincial Councils,
and Local Government

'*My Name Is Cinnamon* takes us on an interesting journey full of adventure and emotions, while introducing the reader to the Indian culture. People of all ages will enjoy reading this lovely book.'

—Samar Mahfouz Barraj, Lebanon
Award-winning writer, playwright, lyricist, poet, and
winner of four Etisalat awards for
Arabic children's literature

'Children will certainly recognise themselves in this character—from not wanting to go to school to friendship challenges and home life. I love how the chapters are rooted in Indian culture and have engaging and interesting titles, relatable to both children and adults.'

—Jennifer Gagner, Madagascar
Curriculum coordinator and secondary school English
teacher, American School of Antananarivo

'From the first pages of the book, the story gets you sucked into its plot with its vivid descriptions. This intimate and well-turned writing style continues throughout the story that unravels, approaching the delicate subject of adoption in a very sensitive, straightforward, and serious way.'

—Giorgos Vlachakis and Eliza Neophytou, Greece
Founders, Eat Dessert First Greece

'Reading Vikas Joshi's *My Name Is Cinnamon* in Cairo was a delight. Vikas is a gifted storyteller. His storytelling is intelligent, heartfelt, and witty and his style is one of companionship and evokes trust.'

—Karim-Yasin Goessinger, Egypt
Founder and director, Cairo Institute of Liberal Arts and Sciences

'When I read it, I was picturing it as clips from a movie. It has a strong cinematic quality.'

—Dr Gulnara Mursalimova, Kazakhstan
Assistant professor and researcher, Kazakh National Academy of Arts

*contd . . .*

'We will always remember Cinnamon and the lessons he unintentionally bestows on us.'

—Dr Kelly Mekdeci, Guyana
Former principal, Georgetown International Academy, Guyana

'I thought this story was beautifully written.'

—Dr Pete Kellet, USA
Professor, Department of Communication Studies, University of North Carolina, USA

'Full of vivid local detail while at the same time portraying childhood experiences and emotions that occur in every culture.'

—Mark Levinson, Israel
Secretary, Israel Association of Writers in English

'The author has made sure to take us on a jaunty ride of the rich tapestry of Indian culture and lifestyle, through a brilliant portrayal of interesting characters, places, and events.'

—Jayant Sharma, Nepal
Author and editor, Sathi literary journal, Nepal

**Disclaimer**

This book is a work of fiction that was inspired by true events. Unless otherwise indicated, all the names, characters, businesses, places, events, and incidents in this book are either the product of the author's imagination or used in a fictitious manner.

# Accolades

1. Skipping Stones Honour Award, 2023, for Multicultural and International Books
2. A3F Literary Award, 2023
3. Asian Literary Society Award, 2023, for Best Debut Fiction
4. Asian Literary Society Certificate of Excellence in Fiction Award, 2023
5. FICCI Publishing Award, 2023, for Best Children's Book (Above 10 Years)
6. Nissim Prize for English Prose, 2023
7. Shortlisted for Valley of Words Award, 2023, for Young Adult Books
8. Longlisted for Binod Kanoria Award, 2023, for Children's Literature
9. Finalist for Eyelands Book Awards, 2023 (Children's Published Books Category)
10. Shortlisted for PragatiE Vichaar Literary Festival Awards, 2024 (Best Debut Fiction – English Category)

# My Name Is CINNAMON

*Vikas Prakash Joshi*

HAY HOUSE

HAY HOUSE INDIA
New Delhi • London • Sydney
Carlsbad, California • New York City

**Hay House Publishers (India) Pvt Ltd**
Muskaan Complex, Plot No. 3, B-2, Vasant Kunj, New Delhi – 110070, India

Hay House LLC, P.O. Box 5100, Carlsbad, CA 92018-5100, USA
Hay House UK Ltd, 1st Floor, Crawford Corner, 91-93 Baker Street, London W1U 6QQ, UK
Hay House Australia Publishing Pty Ltd, 18/36 Ralph St., Alexandria NSW 2015, Australia

Email: contact@hayhouse.co.in
Website: www.hayhouse.co.in

*Illustrated by* Niloufer Wadia



First published by Hay House India, 2022
Reprint, 2025
13 12 11 10 9 8 7 6 5 4

ISBN 978-93-94613-18-8
ISBN 978-93-94613-19-5 (ebook)

Printed at Repro India Limited

FSC www.fsc.org MIX Paper from responsible sources FSC® C047271

Hay House is committed to a sustainable future for our business, our readers and our planet. This book is made from Forest Stewardship Council® certified paper.

Dedication

For my parents, Aai and Baba, and brother Madhavdada.

Also, for my wonderful English school teachers: in particular the late Dr Patrick Fredericks, Dr Kelly Mekdeci, and Mrs Pramila Mathews.

# Contents

*'Books are sometimes windows, offering views of worlds that may be real or imagined, familiar or strange . . . when lighting conditions are just right, however, a window can also be a mirror. Literature transforms human experience and reflects it back to us, and in that reflection we can see our own lives and experiences as part of the larger human experience. Reading, then, becomes a means of self-affirmation, and readers often seek their mirrors in books.'*

—Dr Rudine Sims Bishop

# Introduction

Hi! My name is Cinnamon, and we are soon going to get to know each other quite well. You might be wondering about my unusual nickname. The truth is my name actually isn't Cinnamon. My real name is Roshan Rishikesh Paranjape but when I was very small, my parents dubbed me Cinnamon. It seemed fine at that time but now I am not at all fond of my nickname. To be frank, there are times when I hate it and want to change it to something more stylish. Aside from my nickname, there are a few other things that are a bit different about me. You will come to know about it soon enough. Mitra, I will see you in the coming pages.

## *Chapter 1*

# My Own Face

*'I have wrought my simple plan, if I give one hour of joy, to the boy who's half a man, or the man who's half a boy.'*

—Sir Arthur Conan Doyle

The spectators watched with bated breath and pounding hearts. They bit their nails nervously; this was the moment they all had waited for.

Bathed in Pune's gentle early morning September sunshine, the Khadki Football Ground echoed with raucous, full-throated cries of 'Go DIS!' and 'Come on Royal!' It was the finals of the Pune Under-13 School Football Championship. Cinnamon Paranjape, the goalkeeper for the Diamond International School, nervously adjusted his green football jersey. He said a silent prayer in his mind and put his hands on his knees. He knew how important it was to keep out this penalty kick.

The scoreboard showed 2-1 in favour of the DIS. For the first time in ten years, DIS had a chance to defeat the defending champions Royal National Academy (RNA) and win the championship. Dressed in their trademark maroon shirts, socks, and shorts, the RNA team stood on the left side of the field. On the other side was the class sixth DIS team in their stylish dark green outfits.

Cinnamon looked to the right towards his team's supporters and a noisy green gaggle of parents and friends. Amidst the crowd, he spotted Baba dressed in a green polo T-shirt and jeans, recording on his iPad. Maa, who was sitting next to him in a white kameez and green salwar, shouted enthusiastically, 'Go Cinnamon! Come on, Cinnamon!' She then whistled with two fingers in her mouth. Pallavi, his best friend, was also present and waved a placard with the message: 'East or West, DIS is the best.'

Cinnamon then looked ahead. On the field were his buddies—Captain Harpreet, Chhota Sidhu, their best defender, Onam Kutty, and the rest of the DIS football team. He could also see his coach, Shetty sir, striding anxiously on the sidelines. He saw the tension writ large on their faces. He then took a deep breath and said a prayer.

Rishabh Keswani, RNA's best striker, was all set to take the penalty for the defending champions. He had already scored more goals than anyone else in the tournament. His team members cheered him on. As Rishabh raced up to the ball, coach Shetty's words flashed in Cinnamon's mind: 'Remember, Rishabh scores most of his goals in the top or bottom left-hand corner. That side will be on your right.' Cinnamon took a deep breath and crouched down, his nails digging into his thighs. The audience rose to its feet in anticipation.

*Thump!*

Cinnamon threw himself boldly and confidently to his right and crashed, close to the white frame bars of the goal. For a moment, time stood still for him.

When he scrambled up, Rishabh's face told him everything. His hands and body stung from the sheer force of Rishabh's kick and the crash to the ground, but it didn't matter, for school captain Harpreet was running towards him. 'Congrats, Lambu Das!' shouted Harpreet as he jumped on him and hugged him.

The crowd went berserk and started shouting, 'Congrats, Cinnamon!' and 'Goalkeeper kaisa ho? Cinnamon jaisa ho!' These slogans were music to his ears. After ten years, DIS had won the football championship. Coach Shetty later carried Cinnamon on his shoulders and they did a victory lap with the entire team. Then the team gathered together to pose for photos with the medals around their necks and the huge golden Royal Trophy. Rishabh received the Highest Goal Scorer award while Cinnamon took home the Best Goalkeeper award.

After much back-slapping and high-fiving, they climbed into the school bus. Cinnamon grabbed his favourite window seat. He hummed 'Aashayein' from Iqbal. The breeze blowing on his sweaty face was refreshing.

'Lambu Das, tell me one thing.'

Cinnamon turned to his side to see who was speaking to him. It was Awaneesh or Teacher as they had nicknamed him, digging his nose furiously as if there were diamonds inside. He always dug his nose or ears when thinking hard about something.

'Why one thing, Teacher? I will tell two things.'

'How you became so tall? Your mom and dad are not so lambu. You look also different from them,' said Teacher as he adjusted his spectacles on his thick nose. His fat legs shook as he asked this question.

Cinnamon shrugged. 'Arey, Teacher, your mom and dad are super thin but you became so motu. How come?'

'Don't call me Teacher.'

'Okay Teacher, I won't call you Teacher. I will call you Motu.' There were guffaws all around.

'Shut up, Lambu Kali Das.'

'Okay, Motuji.' Everyone followed the suit and there were cries of 'Motu! Motu!' in the bus. Teacher took a pen and threw it at Cinnamon, who ducked, and it safely sailed out the window. Pulling out the small pencil he always kept in his hair, Cinnamon threw it back in retort. To Cinnamon's satisfaction, the pencil deposited itself in Teacher's arm. It was impossible for anything thrown at Teacher not to hit him, there was so much of him.

'Ouch!' Teacher winced, more in surprise than pain. The boys burst into laughter.

When the bus dropped Cinnamon home, his heart jumped to see the red Skoda Octavia parked in the society parking lot. Maa was home before 7 p.m. for a change. He found Baba and Maa sitting in Baba's home office. Maa put aside the voluminous red legal tome she was studying and gave him a rib-crunching bear hug.

'Abhinandan!' Baba said and then gave him a high-five and clapped him on his back.

At dinner, they had puri, amras, and batatyachi bhaji. Cinnamon described the game, his eyes shining with excitement. 'We knew that Rishabh had to be kept under control, so our team marked him very well. Harpreet scored two goals before the first half. And then Rishabh scored a goal. I had my heart in my mouth till the end. The penalty kick was so exciting.'

'Harpreet scored two goals but you saved many more. Sardar aur asardar. A winning combo,' quipped Baba.

'In school, I was very good at sports, Cinnamon. My son, after all,' Maa observed as she patted his head.

'Basundhara Ghosal Paranjape, you came first in every subject in school. You were also a sports champion. Remind me which school you went to?'

Maa ignored Baba's comments and concentrated on scooping up the amras with her flaky golden puris. But Baba's face showed that there had been a contact between Maa's foot and his leg.

'Maa, whose face do I have? Yours or Baba's?'

'Someone in your class said something?' Maa asked after a pause. She carefully touched her black hair, streaked with silver and cut in bangs—her latest hairstyle. She had swarthy, oily skin and was short.

Baba chuckled and stretched out his skinny, fair legs. There was a twinkle in his grey-green eyes. 'Why do you need to look like us? You are good-looking as you are.'

Before Cinnamon went to bed, he looked in the mirror. He started making weird faces at the boy opposite him. He opened his mouth as wide as he could, squinted his eyes, and pulled his front teeth out like a beaver. He stuck his tongue out and put fingers in both his ears before puffing up his cheeks and rolling his eyeballs. He scrunched his face into the most hideous expression. He made his nose into a pig's snout.

He stared at his reflection. Though it was the same face he saw every morning, these days he looked at it more and more often. Sharp cheekbones, dark skin, crinkly hair, and chocolate-coloured eyes which held a curious, mischievous look, stared back at him. Yes, he, Cinnamon, officially named Roshan Rishikesh Paranjape, did look different from his parents, especially his father. 'You look different.' The statement echoed in his mind. A statement which he had heard many times before.

It was true. I don't have my father's face or mother's face. Which was hardly surprising; after all, he was an adopted child. I have my own face, he thought. And that was all that mattered.

He fell asleep, dreaming of being the Indian goalkeeper in the Football World Cup final against Brazil. The match was played in front of the prime minister and other dignitaries, top Bollywood actors, Baba and Maa and, of course, Pallavi aka Palli, who kept energetically waving the Indian flag throughout the match. The crowd kept blowing vuvuzelas. In the end, the Brazilian team was defeated as they could not put a single goal past Cinnamon.

The Indian players got gold medals, trophies, and jumbo-sized cheques. But one special prize was reserved for Cinnamon. The prime minister handed Cinnamon the Player of the Match prize. They weighed Cinnamon on a giant scale or thulabharam and then gave him a huge, rich silky fruit and nut chocolate bar equal to his weight and size. A car had to be hired to bring it home.

## *Chapter 2*

# An Upset Tummy

Mornings in A-28, Belvedere Towers, Koregaon Park, were always buzzing with numerous activities.

The Bose speaker in the living room started its work for the day and played the Marathi bhajan, 'Utha Utha Ho Sakalik', which was the family's morning wake-up tune. Cinnamon yawned, turned in his bed, and then snuggled under the bedsheet. He wished he could hit the snooze button.

'Cinnamon baby, time to get up!' Maa said while sprinkling water droplets on him.

'Don't do that Maa!' he grumbled, before his feet reached for the red slippers near his bed.

'Baby, say your prayers before you take a bath,' she reminded him. He had told Maa several times not to call him 'Baby', but Maa was rebellious as always. Next time, he would have to be stricter, he thought. He recited 'Vakratunda Mahakaya' and 'Sada Sarvada Yog Tujha' from memory before going off for a bath.

The smell of agarbattis and the sound of Maa reciting Sanskrit verses in her pooja room filled the flat. 'Baba, why don't you have to go to school in the morning?' asked Cinnamon critically while drinking hot milk with Nesquik powder at the breakfast table. On the menu was poha, sausages, and jam toast.

Baba looked at him over his glass of freshly squeezed orange juice. 'Don't you want some bread to go with all that butter and jam?'

'Baba, why can't I stay at home, like you?'

'I went to school when I was young. There is no need to go now.'

'But I also have gone to school so many times. Why can't I stay at home?'

'I don't have any objection if you stay at home,' Baba replied smugly and then went back to sipping his juice. Cinnamon wondered what the catch was. 'You have to convince Maa and your teachers, that's all.' Cinnamon made a face. He knew that wasn't happening any time soon.

Baba finished his juice and went off for a swim at the complex pool below. The school bus normally came by 7:30 a.m., so Cinnamon and Maa were always ready and waiting outside the gate by 7:15 a.m. But today, things took a different turn.

Suddenly, Cinnamon cried out in heartrending agony, 'Oh, my stomach! Owww! Aai gaa! Aaaa!' Maa rushed him upstairs and to the bathroom, where he spent the next twenty minutes. 'Maa, my stomach is paining so much. I can't tell you,' he said when he came out, before lying down on the bed. He gripped his stomach and grimaced, pain clearly written all over his face.

'Cinnamon, what happened? Are you okay?'

'No. No! Aaaa!' Meena bai, their cook, rushed into the room.

'Khoka, are you okay?' repeated Maa and put her hand on Cinnamon's forehead.

Cinnamon shook his head, writhing in indescribable agony. Hearing Cinnamon's cry for help, their neighbour, Mrs Dastoor, also hurried over. She was a good neighbour, always ready to help with tea powder, sugar, and good advice, especially when nobody asked for it.

'Poor child. Can't say, ya, about the food these days. Must be milk powder and plastic-shastic,' observed Mrs Dastoor, patting her belly.

Maa scolded Meena bai about the food. 'Kaku, I am preparing the food in front of you! How can you ask whether it was stale? Don't I eat the same food?' Meena bai retorted. She went back to the kitchen. The sounds of the ladle being banged in the cooking pot were evident. Cinnamon stayed home and had Eno, buttermilk, and medicines.

A few days later, it happened again and this time, it was even worse than before. Baba and Maa took Cinnamon to Dr Ubale, who ran a clinic nearby. He examined Cinnamon thoroughly—pressed his stomach, took his temperature, and made him open his mouth, take deep breaths, and say 'Aaah' several times with a stethoscope on his chest and back.

Dr Ubale was tall, fair in complexion, and completely bald. His round, massive head reminded Cinnamon of a boiled egg. Cinnamon had nicknamed him 'Dr Ubalahua Anda' (Dr Boiled Egg). Dr Ubalahua Anda wrote a string of indecipherable scribbles on his notepad and handed it back to him with a flourish. Baba's eyebrows, which generally preferred to lie down, started climbing after looking at the prescription. 'You may get these at Classic Medicals down the road. Tell him I sent you.'

'Does my son really need so many medicines?' asked Baba suspiciously. 'It's only a stomach ache.'

Dr Ubalahua Anda pursed his lips. 'I am a doctor with over forty years of experience. Don't tell me what to prescribe and what not to,' he said acerbically in Marathi. 'These are for your son,' he then added, handing over the prescription with a flourish.

But these life-saving medicines prescribed by a doctor with over forty years of experience had no impact. Cinnamon repeatedly had stomach pains even after taking them. It didn't matter what the breakfast was—bacon and toast, sabudana khichadi, chicken sausages, upma, poha, or even plain curd rice with salt—Cinnamon's stomach issues continued. It was a mystery that only Sherlock Holmes or Hercule Poirot could have solved.

Saturday rolled around. Cinnamon was deep in the adventure storybook, *Fursungicha Faster Fene* by B.R. Bhagwat. He found written Marathi initially long-winded and tough going but was now getting the hang of it. Baba insisted he read Marathi books whenever possible.

'Roshan, come here,' Maa called out to him.

'Maa, what happened? Is there anything wrong, Maa?'

'Roshan, don't Maa me. Please come here,' she replied. Maa calling him Roshan was a sign that it was at a category-2 level of seriousness.

Cinnamon dragged himself to his parents' bedroom. Baba was sitting there with one hand stroking his thinning hair. They both had the 'We want to have a word with you' look. Cinnamon's heart sank further.

'Cinnamon, your stomach aches and you constantly going to the bathroom in the morning have happened many times. And by the time we reach your school, you have already missed the first and even second periods. Your principal has also spoken to us about it. At this rate, you won't be able to give your mid-terms.'

'We have also seen,' continued Maa inexorably, like a true lawyer, 'that you always develop these stomach pains only on Mondays, Tuesdays, and Fridays.'

Cinnamon looked at Maa's bonsai plants on the windowsill for support. They looked back at him sympathetically but remained silent. 'No! That's not true!'

'Yes, it is. And your first period on these days is math,' she said, clinching the argument. She adjusted the red and white shakha-pola (Bengali bangles) on her wrist. There was silence.

'Uh . . . uh . . . well . . .'

'We know you are struggling with math. Mrs Godbole says that you are not keeping up with the class. Even the homework, Palli does it and you copy it. She says you do sketches and write poems in class.'

'No, that's not true,' he cried out.

She opened his math notebook and displayed the pages which were mostly blank except the ones at the back. They were quite full but not with math sums. There were an enthralling kaleidoscope of simple pencil sketch illustrations of different kinds, that included chubby Sundar, Palli with her cute freckles and, short and stocky Onam Kutty. There were also sketches of tall and skinny Rashi, the class topper, with her long thin arm always raised to answer or ask a question, their classroom, and Kadubole ma'am herself.

He looked at his illustrations with admiration. They were damn good, even if he said so himself.

'I hate Mrs Kadubole's classes,' he exclaimed with genuine emotion. 'In fact, everyone hates her, except Teacher, Onam Kutty, and Dhapnya.' He puckered his lips as if he was biting a lemon to show how kadu she was.

'Cinnamon, don't use such rude nicknames for your teachers! We know that you don't like Mrs Godbole. So, we have decided that I will tutor you instead.' Well, it wasn't exactly an exciting prospect but it was way better than another Mrs Godbole. Cinnamon looked at Baba hopefully, but his blank face—blank as most of his math notebook pages—showed that he was going to be as useful as the bonsai plants.

'It's up to you, Cinnamon,' said Maa. Up to you, in parent's language, meant that you can do whatever you want, as long as it's what we want you to do.

'Mrs Godbole said that she will always be there for you if there is any problem,' added Baba, suddenly rediscovering his vocal cords.

That was the whole point. She being there for him was the problem, but Baba and Maa did not understand this at all, he thought with a sigh.

When Cinnamon was back in class on Monday, he found there had been other unwelcome changes. His seat had been shifted from the back, where he sat with Onam Kutty, Harpreet, and Palli, to the front row, next to Martand, the math topper.

They were studying the concept of percentages. Mrs Godbole noticed him towering over Martand. Mrs Godbole was short, plump, wheat-complexioned and wore glasses. When she was serious— which was most of the time—she kept her glasses on. When she smiled—which was very rarely— she would always take off her spectacles. You could either see her smile or her spectacles but not both of them together.

She looked at Cinnamon and smiled . . . a smile that that had all the genuineness of a mass forwarded Diwali WhatsApp greeting. 'Are you feeling fine today?' she asked.

'Yes ma'am, I am fine.'

'No early morning loose motion issues, I hope?' Her nostrils flared. The class tittered and Roshan grimaced. You are not supposed to talk about somebody's loose motion in front of the entire class. Wasn't this a part of the manual that every teacher supposedly got?

'No, ma'am.' To his surprise, she did not pursue the matter and the first few days of the week went by smoothly.

Friday morning came around and for the first time, Cinnamon gave himself permission to breathe.

Little did he know, it was only the lull before the storm.

In the class, Kadubole ma'am's practice was to write a math question on the blackboard and read it out loud to the entire class. She then would call a hapless student to solve the problem.

'Solve the following problem,' said Kadubole. 'Shashwat has Rs 400. He spends 3/4 on sardines and ¼ on prawns. 1 kg of prawns cost Rs 150 and 1 kg of sardines cost Rs 50. How many kgs of prawns and sardines does he buy?'

She looked all around the room. Her eyes darted from student to student. They all tried to avoid making eye contact. Cinnamon unsuccessfully tried to tuck his long legs and arms into the chair. Without a moment's hesitation, she sweetly shattered his life into a thousand splendid fragments. 'Roshan, would you please come forward and solve the problem.'

Would you please, thought Cinnamon annoyed. As if he had a choice. He came forward and read through the problem carefully. Shashwat was a dumb guy. Why not spend all the money on prawns, instead of buying rubbery, tasteless sardines? Gross. Shashwat had obviously never had Maa's Sunday special chingri malai prawn curry. His mouth watered just thinking about it. But soon, Mrs Kadubole brought him back to reality by handing him the chalk.

'Ma'am, I have one doubt about this sum,' ventured Cinnamon, after profound contemplation.

'Yes, Roshan beta, where is the difficulty?'

'Why only sardines and prawns? Doesn't Shashwat need rice and vegetables also? Also, since prawns are tastier than sardines, why doesn't he only buy prawns? Doesn't that make more sense?' There was a ripple of laughter through the class that subsided with a glance from Mrs Godbole.

With her Diwali Whatsapp forward smile firmly in place, she said, 'Roshan Paranjape, solve the problem in front of you please.'

Cinnamon silently prayed and after some intense calculations, handed over the chalk. Mrs Godbole's jaw collapsed like a bridge in heavy rain when she saw the board. It read: Rs 400/150+50 = 400/200 = 2. Of this 2, ¾ are spent on sardines and ¼ on prawns hence, the total amount of sardines Shashwat purchased = 1.5 kg and prawns = 0.5 kg.

After completing the answer, Cinnamon stepped back. He was proud of how quickly he had done the calculation. He was crestfallen to see that Mrs Kadubole was still agape. He could hear some students giggling.

'Is there anything wrong in the calculation, ma'am?' he asked.

'Y-Y-You m-may return to your desk, Roshan,' she spluttered.

Cinnamon returned to his desk, his normally erect, sturdy shoulders drooping. No subject troubled him the way math did. No wonder then, his math paper was always full of countless red splashes, like the old T-shirt in which he played Holi with his colony friends.

Cinnamon thought about how much he hated Shashwat. He also hated Raman who took a loan of Rs 9,768 and forgot to work out the annual interest of 9 per cent per year or the 22 fishermen of Nagercoil who deposited money in accounts and then couldn't calculate what the total amount was. Why do they expect me to calculate for them? he thought angrily.

While walking on the school grounds with Pallavi, Cinnamon asked her, 'Don't you think math was basically invented to torture us?'

Palli thumped him on the back in hearty agreement. 'True yaar. Why do you even need to study it for so many years when everyone anyway has a calculator in their pockets?'

A few days later, when he came home, he saw certain UAOs (unattractive academic objects) on his desk. They looked boring, deadly, and extremely avoidable, exactly like Mrs Kadubole's math problems. He didn't want to ruin his day any further so he kept them in the desk drawer, safe from everyone's sight, and busied himself with the other homework.

The next day morning, before school, his deepest, darkest suspicions were indeed confirmed. 'Cinnamon baby, did you have a look at the books?' Maa asked as she sprinkled golden coloured sev on top of her upma.

He opened his eyes wide. 'Which books, Maa?' He tried to sound innocent but Maa wasn't buying it.

'The books on your table, Khoka.' It was Maa's favourite trick to add 'Khoka' or baby at the end of a sentence to convince him to do something he didn't want to. It was highly diabolical and unscrupulous.

Without any mercy, she squeezed a helpless lemon and the juice spilt all over her upma. She went on equally mercilessly, squeezing his happiness too, drop by drop. 'We will use these to study math together. The books focus on how math can be fun. They teach it in a very different way, an entertaining way. These books are not like your typical school math textbooks.'

'Wookay.'

'Won't it be so fun?'

'Yes, Maa, what fun it will be! Yay, yippee,' Cinnamon said sarcastically. He groaned and made a face.

'Cinnamon, I don't like this attitude.'

'Woo-kaay, Maa. Lol.'

Maa made it a point to sit with Cinnamon and help him with his math homework. On Sunday evenings, they prepared for the full week ahead. Baba intervened only when Cinnamon simply couldn't grasp something. Thanks to Maa and countless cups of chocolate milk from Baba and Meena bai, he managed to get his marks in math up to at least a passing percentage. There were finally some blues as well in his examination papers and not just reds.

Cinnamon wondered sometimes why he found math so challenging, when Baba and Maa could apparently easily sail through it.

One Sunday afternoon, Cinnamon slept off after lunch. When he awoke, he heard low murmuring voices from his parents' bedroom. He went towards the door and then quietly kneeled behind it, putting his eye to the keyhole. Baba, as always, had his feet stretched out in front, while Maa was sitting on the chair in front of him. Baba's back was towards the door and he could see his father's wavy black hair.

'Cinnamon really struggles with mathematics. He struggles to understand even basic concepts. His math teacher told me on the phone that he is scared of the subject. I always came first in my class in math. His teacher also complains that he doesn't pay attention,' he heard Maa's voice.

He pressed his ear to the door to hear what Baba had to say. 'I don't think we should get so worked up about one subject. As it is, we are coaching him, so he will improve. He does very well in history, English, social studies, sports, and art,' Baba said. 'Initially, I struggled a lot with English, especially speaking it, as I came from a Marathi medium school. Now when people hear me speak English, they even ask me whether I went to a convent school,' he said emphatically. 'Imagine that.'

'Maths at this stage is very easy. If he finds this tough, then what will he do in higher classes? I am sure he can do better. Math along with English is the foundation for all subjects,' she retorted. 'If you master these subjects, you can pass anything.'

'As I said, math is only one subject. You know, Basundhara, math is not an easy subject. In fact, even now, after being an engineer, I struggle with many complex calculations. For example, I still can't figure out how many times you have made fish curry and kosha mangsho since we got married. Or how many saris you have and how many more you plan to buy. I tried a few times but I couldn't manage. It was too difficult,' Baba quipped.

Maa slapped Baba on the shoulder. 'Stop making everything a joke.'

His father remained silent for a few minutes after this remark. Then, slowly, he said, 'I agree math is an important subject. Well, we can only give him the best possible tuition and education at the best school. Now you are coaching him in math, and he will improve as time goes by. But let's face it. He has his own strengths and weakness. At the end of the day, it is what it is. No point in expecting him to be as good in math as we used to be. There are many other things he can be good at, and is actually.'

'He can be as good at math as anyone. He is such an intelligent boy,' said Maa with a note of pride in her voice. The word 'tuitions' hung in the air, threateningly. Cinnamon rushed back to the room, wishing he hadn't overheard the conversation. It was true, he reflected. Math problems seemed like trying to read something in Russian or Arabic. He just had to look at all those signs and numbers and his head would start swimming. He wrote a few lines about it in his notebook:

Teacher, teacher . . . boring right?
In the classroom of the fright
What inhumane hand or eye
Could frame such monotonous syllabi?

When he did his homework, studied his textbooks, or gazed at the shiny globe on his study table, sometimes certain questions crossed Cinnamon's mind. As an adopted child, he occasionally wondered about how his birth parents were when they were young.

Were they not good at math like him or did they excel in it? Were they good at history, drawing, and English? Were they fond of drama and sports? What were they like? I would really like to ask them, Cinnamon thought. If I get just one chance, I would ask them that and so many other things as well.

*Chapter 3*

# KRISHNA AND KARNA

It is Newton's fifth law that when a teacher steps out of a primary school class for more than a decent period of time, somebody starts singing. The fifth standard class at Diamond International School, Koregaon Park, was no exception to this eternal rule.

Cinnamon clutched the long stainless-steel ruler like a mike in front of the class. The other twenty students noisily and tunelessly joined in as he belted out 'Lakdi Ki Kathi' at the top of his voice. It was a welcome break from the environmental science class. Pallavi joined him as the female lead.

Just as the horse was bolting, the EVS teacher, Mrs Arora, came back into the classroom. 'Settle down, horses! Roshan and Palli, take your seats,' she said. The class went back to the lesson.

When the class ended, students started filing out noisily. Just as Cinnamon was about to exit the classroom, the teacher called out his name. 'Roshan.'

'Yes ma'am?'

'Where do you stay?'

'Koregaon Park, ma'am.'

'Wah. You like singing?'

'Ummm . . . I love singing.'

'I am sure even Gulzar in Mumbai would have heard you singing his lyrics.'

'Really, ma'am?'

'Haanji.'

Cinnamon blushed and looked down at the ground. 'Thank you, ma'am,' he finally muttered.

A thought struck Mrs Arora. 'How did you get the nickname, Cinnamon? Everyone calls you that.'

'My parents love to add cinnamon to everything. In tea, cakes, pastries, and rolls . . . in everything. I couldn't pronounce the word cinnamon so I called it cimmanum or cinnamum or even cimmamom. So, they dubbed me Cinnamon.' His words were accompanied by a frown. 'But I don't like my nickname anymore. I want to change it but I guess it's too late for it now.'

She nodded in agreement and then asked, 'Are they fond of music, like you?'

'No ma'am. They don't like music,' he replied. 'I mean they do like it but not this kind of music.' He wildly gesticulated with his hands, trying to explain what kind of music he was referring to. The teacher gave a knowing smile. 'It's only me. Maybe my tummy-mummy liked this kind of music.'

'Your tummy mummy?'

'Yes. I am adopted.'

Mrs Arora fiddled with her dangling silver earrings. After smiling a little too long, she said, 'Okay, wonderful, Roshan. Keep it up. You can go now.'

Baba and Maa never hid from Cinnamon, or anyone else, that he was adopted. It was as much an accepted part of his life as his alert brown eyes and long, muscular legs. When he was about two years old, Maa sat him down and told him a beautiful story. She read it to him from a slim Bengali book. Baba was also there in the room. The story was about the ancient city of Mathura, near Delhi, where Vasudev and Devaki had eight children. 'The eighth child was Krishna. When Krishna was born, there was heavy rain. Vasudev took the baby in a wicker basket to the house of Nanda. He placed him with Nanda, a cowherd, for his protection. Lord Krishna grew up with his adoptive parents,' narrated Maa with dramatic voice variations and hand movements.

Baba then told another story in Marathi in a silky, smooth voice. In the story, a charioteer finds a baby in a basket floating in a river. The charioteer and his wife, Adirath and Radha, did not have children of their own. 'Little did they know that the boy was the son of princess Kunti and Surya Dev. They named him Karna. He grew up to be a brave and fearless warrior.'

'So, you see, Cinnamon, some children come home in some ways and others in other ways, but every one of them is equally special,' Maa concluded.

Baba said, 'When we went to the adoption agency, they said that the boy looks different from you. But that didn't matter to us.'

When Cinnamon was four, Baba and Maa took him to the hospital where he was born. The hospital was located in the congested and heaving Kusalkar road area of Pune. They also took him to the adoption centre, near one of Pune's biggest hospitals, when he was five, and again when he was six. Baba told him the story of the day they adopted him. 'Cinnamon, the day we went to bring you home, was the most memorable day of my life. It was not only your Maa and me who went to the adoption centre. Aaji, ajoba, dada moshay, and didi maa also came along. I finally understood what it was like to be the captain of the Indian cricket team. We only had a Maruti Zen at that time, so we arranged two autorickshaws additionally to take everyone.'

He continued with eyes twinkling, 'It rained the previous night and early that morning as well and we felt it to be a good omen. Later, we organised a get together at a small mangal karyalaya for all the people on your homecoming day. So many people came home that we had to shift it to a much bigger hall nearby.' Cinnamon really loved to hear this story again and again, and each time Baba added extra details.

Baba and Maa always supported him and let everyone know that he was adopted, so that he had no sense of shame or embarrassment. He saw it as a natural part of his identity. As Cinnamon grew older, he sometimes stared into the bathroom mirror, trying to imagine what his father and mother must have looked like. Did his swarthy skin, impressive height, and sharp nose and cheekbones come from his father? Did he get his loud laughter and voice from his mother? Where did they live and what did they do? Wherever he travelled, he looked at people and thought occasionally whether any one of them was his father or mother.

On one occasion, when he was about six years old, he asked Baba, 'Baba, if my birth mother were to come and ask to take me back, what would you do?'

'We don't know where she is and she doesn't know where we are either. So that can't happen. Moreover, we love you and we won't ever let you go.'

Later, when he was around seven, he had more questions. He asked his parents, 'What did my birth father and mother look like? Are they tall like me?'

'We don't know, Cinnamon,' they said patiently.

'How come?'

'We have never met them.'

'Why did they leave me? How could they do that?' he cried out. Baba and Maa hugged him tightly and kissed him. 'Was there something wrong with me?' he persisted.

'They didn't give you up. There was, and is, nothing wrong with you. Your birth parents must have had some very good reasons and that is why they had to take the decision they did.' But somewhere, this question remained in his mind.

Nivedita tai and Yatin dada lived on the first floor of their building. They were regulars at the jogging track with Baba. They often came back home together, drenched in sweat, with Yatin and Nivedita always laughing and Baba recounting some story or the other.

One day, at the breakfast table, Maa told Baba with a smile, 'You know, Nivedita is expecting.'

Baba chuckled. 'Well, that was quick,' he said.

Cinnamon didn't know what Nivedita was expecting but he did see Nivedita tai's otherwise flat stomach grow and grow with no end in sight. It troubled him but nobody was bothered about it. On the contrary, they all seemed very happy. They even patted her on the stomach.

He asked Maa, 'Maa, what's happening to Nivedita tai? Why doesn't she do something? She will burst open!'

'Khoka, she will do something soon.'

Then, one day, Nivedita tai suddenly disappeared and so did Yatin dada. Their flat was locked. After a week, the doorbell rang. It was Yatin with a box of golden kesari pedhas in his hands. He was beaming as if he had won on *Kaun Banega Crorepati* or become the prime minister of India.

Maa came up to the door. 'Oho! Congratulations!'

exclaimed Maa and hugged him. Baba reached out and hugged him too. 'What is her name?'

'Anvee.'

'Beautiful name. Welcome to the club, sir. Congratulations once again,' said Baba. Cinnamon didn't completely understand why Baba was congratulating Yatin dada if Anvee had come out of Nivedita tai's tummy. What did he have to do with it? Cinnamon wondered.

Every Sunday evening, Maa invariably gave a head massage to Cinnamon with mustard oil. Baba had tried to get her to switch to coconut oil but to no avail. Though Cinnamon hated the smell, he always loved the warm and fuzzy sensation it left when she finished her massage.

'Head massage is good for blood flow and intelligence, you know,' she declared. 'Your dadu and didi maa gave us regular head massages with castor oil when we were growing up. That's why we turned out so well, I say. It's a must actually, for all children.'

Cinnamon knew where this conversation was going, so he decided to divert it. 'Maa, I have a question,' he asked.

'Yes.'

'Anvee came out of Nivedita tai's tummy?'

'Of course, baby.'

'So, you and Baba also came out of didi maa and aaji's tummies? And others too?'

'Yes, even we did,' she reassured.

'But I didn't come out of here?' he said, touching Maa's tummy. 'I wasn't in here?'

'Not from my tummy. You were in my mind,' she said, quoting Tagore.

'Whose stomach did I come from?'

'Your birth mother's.'

He looked at his own tummy and imagined a baby inside. He imagined himself inside a tummy, arms and legs and all. What an ugly sight it must have been. 'Maa, it must be so painful,' Cinnamon cried out.

'Yes, it is painful at that time but then once the baby is born, the pain goes.'

'Don't you think that shows how nice I am? I came without causing you any trouble.'

Maa cupped his chin and laughed. Then she carried on with the head massage, humming to herself.

*Chapter 4*

# Batman and Kosha Mangsho

From Monday to Friday, Meena bai ran the house but on Saturday and Sunday, Maa took over.

A barrage of loud instructions on Saturday morning showed that the weekly handover was in full swing. 'Cinnamon, once you brush your teeth and get dressed, come and help me grind the dry and wet masalas. Meena bai, please prepare the marinade for the mutton. And the food for Saheb. Rishi, please load the washing machine and collect the clothes from the istriwala,' she instructed.

'Yes, boss,' remarked Baba.

'Meena bai, has the mutton been properly marinated? Have the onions, tomatoes, and potatoes been cut into small pieces, like I told you last time also?'

'Yes, tai,' came the response by Meena bai.

'Did you pressure cook the mutton for at least seven whistles?'

'Yes, tai.'

'Did you make the vegetarian dishes in separate vessels? Else Saheb will shout.'

'Yes, tai.' She giggled at the idea of Saheb 'shouting' at anyone.

The weekend was also special for another reason: Maa always cooked the Sunday lunch. It was something that everyone had been eagerly waiting for. While Meena bai certainly helped with the grinding and chopping, Maa was the undisputed head chef. The menu consisted of a wide variety of dishes that included tambda or pandhra rassa, pork vindaloo, or chingri malai curry along with tasty vegetarian options for Baba. But her favourite—as well as Cinnamon's and Meena bai's—was the kosha mangsho.

Of course, with Maa taking an interest in the house again, everyone had to jump around and make themselves useful. Maa dusted and tended to her bonsai plants, Baba did the laundry, and Cinnamon folded and refolded the clothes in the cupboard. Meena bai used the mop vigorously till the house looked spick and span. Later that day, a bansuri artist came home to teach Baba the flute and Cinnamon went off for football coaching and art classes.

On Sunday, Manik dropped by. Manik went to the same drawing class as Cinnamon and was a year older than him. In the morning, the entire family along with Manik played scrabble. Manik and Maa teamed up against Baba and Cinnamon. Initially, Maa's team was ahead. Then suddenly, Baba formed a long word. Cinnamon stumbled trying to pronounce the word. 'Dis . . . combo . . . bulate.'

'Ooo! Cheating. Cheating, Rishi! There's no word like discombobulate,' shouted Maa. She raised her arms and did a little jig. 'Our team wins!'

'There certainly is.' Baba swiped his phone and showed it to her.

She read it, twisted her mouth, and put on a 'I am not impressed' look on her face. 'Not bad. I see you have started the "one word per day" service on your phone,' Maa said.

'You are not the only one who knows long English words, Mrs Ghosal. We Marathi medium students are not less than anyone.'

Eventually, Baba and Cinnamon won the game.

At lunchtime, Cinnamon placed everything on the table, taking care that Baba's plate was kept well away from the mutton and fish. For Baba, there was shenga in black masala, slices of crisp begun bhaja, and hot yellow varan with masala bhat.

'Meena bai didn't come again today?' asked Baba.

'Her mame bhau is not well, apparently,' murmured Maa.

'Again? Boss, last week her ajoba had some issue. Before that, her husband had a life-threatening ailment. Now her mame bhau is sick. It seems only men in her family fall sick, and that too only on weekends and public holidays.'

'Rishi, we all need one or two days off a week. Please let it be. Look, your veg delicacies are there,' Maa said, pointing to them with one finger. 'We lucky carnivores get to eat all this yummy stuff.'

'Mrs Ghosal, I am happy with my ghas phus. Your stinky fish and goat meat don't tempt me.'

After such a sumptuous lunch, the only thing possible was to eat something sweet. Baba gave everyone his favourite sandwich ice creams as dessert. The crunch of the hard chocolate with the soft melting vanilla inside was simply bliss. Baba and Maa retired to their room and Cinnamon and Manik went to the flat's balcony. Cinnamon sat on the parapet, while Manik sat on a chair in front. Cinnamon could faintly hear Maa snoring from the room and wondered how Baba could sleep so soundly despite that ridiculous racket. He filed it away in his 'Questions to ask later' folder.

'Maa made me put up a few clothes on the line a

few days ago. It's already bad that she makes me cut vegetables, but putting up clothes, that too banyan and underwear?' Cinnamon told Manik. Seeing that he had got Manik's attention, Cinnamon continued, now more animatedly, 'So, what happened that day, Manik da, was that I forgot to clip the underwear properly. It was a very windy day. You know how it is. Bed sheets or jeans don't fly away easily, but some clothes . . .' Manik giggled which gave Cinnamon all the more encouragement to continue with his story. 'I had gone to sleep after putting them on the line. When I woke up, I saw some clothes had been blown off by the wind. They had fallen in the drain behind the apartment building. It was so embarrassing to go and pick them up in front of everyone.'

'C'mon, Cinnamon, it was only your underwear. It's not something major,' Manik responded.

'No, no! Hear me out first. This wasn't the end of my misery. Two very small, white VIP Frenchie underwear and one very big, red-and-black checked boxer with some Batman images on it were lying in the drain. Luckily, they were all dry. I knew the small ones were mine and assumed the other one was Baba's. So, I brought them home and clipped his boxer on the line. The next morning, Baba had to pack clothes for his trip to Ahmedabad so he started taking the clothes off the line. I was in my room. That is when I heard him shouting very loudly.' Mimicking Baba's nasal, high-pitched tone which he resorted to every time he was very amused or angry about something, Cinnamon said, 'Where the hell did these new Batman boxers come from? I never wear such funny boxers! Who brought this here? I then heard Maa and Baba laughing. I thought both of them would die laughing. I heard Baba saying that I must have picked it up by accident. Maa asked me later whether I had picked it up, but I kept denying it. It was way too embarrassing.'

Manik burst into laughter. 'Cinnamon, dumbo, don't you at least check before picking up things?'

'Stop laughing Manik da! I really felt terrible.'

After a pause, Manik asked, 'Champion, did you ever find out who it belongs to?'

'I think it belongs to Prashant bhaiya, our neighbour in A-30, that chubby guy who is always talking on his hands-free. You know him, right?'

Manik nodded his head. 'He works in IT na. But how do you know it was his? Did you ask him?'

'Well, a few days later, he came to give us his house key in the evening, since he was going out. He told Baba that there was a thief on the prowl in the society and that he would speak about it at the next society meeting. He stressed that we need to have armed guards, biometric scanning, CCTVs, anti-terrorist software and whatnot. Then he said the thief had come to his flat but luckily had only managed to steal a pair of old boxers. Next time, he warned, it could be something much more important.'

'What did uncle say?'

'What he always says. The way things are going these days, you can never tell what will happen. So be careful.'

'So where is it now? Don't tell me you kept them!'

'I don't know. It was a pair of old boxers and not the Kohinoor diamond or something. So, anyway, we have strayed from the topic. Why do you think my parents make me do so many chores?'

'Do you really want to know why your parents ask you to do so many chores?' Manik asked.

Cinnamon nodded.

Manik dropped his voice to whisper and said, 'Actually, your parents didn't really want a child at all. They just wanted someone who could do all the chores at home. They are then going to fatten you up and eat you up when you get older and fleshier. Like cannibals or as it happens in the zombie movies.'

'Why didn't they hire someone to do the chores then?' Cinnamon inquired.

'Why would they? You were totally free!' Manik said, rubbing his forefinger and thumb to drive home the point. 'You better not gain too much weight, kid, or you will become fat and then they will eat you up faster.'

Cinnamon stared at his muscular arms and legs. Is that why Baba and Maa were feeding him so much? He also thought about Meena bai. She was becoming rounder and rounder. He had to warn her too before it was too late!

'I will ask Baba and Maa about this,' he said, mustering up whatever courage he had.

'No, no . . . don't do that!' Manik screamed. Cinnamon was surprised. Why was Manik da suddenly so alarmed?

Later that evening at tea, he asked Maa, 'What's a slave?'

'Wow, Cinnamon! Your vocabulary is really improving.'

'Tell na, Maa.'

'Who taught you this word?'

'Manik da. He said when you decided to get me, you did it because you were looking for a slave to do all the chores for free. He also said that you are fattening me up because you wanted to eat me up later.'

'Manik is a huge movie fan. Must have picked these ideas from there,' said Baba, finally breaking the silence.

Maa's nostrils flared. 'I have never heard anything more ridiculous than this!' She pursed her lips till they became a dangerously thin red line.

'I will talk to him, Basundhara,' Baba said and placed his hand on her shoulder.

'No, I want to,' she said.

Baba shook his head with a slight smile. 'Let me talk to that deed shaana tomorrow and set him straight,' he said, with a tone of finality.

Cinnamon never knew how Baba 'set straight' Manik da the following morning, but that was the last he ever heard of the joke. Manik da also became very cautious about saying anything in front of him.

Later, Baba and Maa told him the more detailed story of his adoption. They sat together in his room and narrated it to him. They both had photo albums with them. Maa opened the photo albums. They had photos of him as a baby, swaddled in baby clothes. 'These are the photos at the adoption agency,' Baba said. Then he opened another album. 'These are the photos from the day you came home.' They also explained how different children came into families in different ways and that there were many kinds of families, but all children were equally precious.

Cinnamon liked hearing the details of how he was brought home, and in particular, of the day he was brought home. He would often ask Maa, 'What was the day like when you brought me home like?' She would patiently tell him the story every time he asked.

With time, Cinnamon started feeling more comfortable about the fact that he was adopted. Baba and Maa took every measure to normalise the concept of adoption. Every year, the family celebrated World Adoption Day on November 9. They also joined a group comprising of adoptive parents. Once a month, the group organised a get together and visited places of historical and cultural importance like Shaniwar Wada, Aga Khan Palace, Lal Mahal, and the Kelkar Museum. After interacting with so many adopted children, Cinnamon realised that being adopted wasn't something unusual. But every once in a while, somebody or something would come along, that would bring out the negative perception that many people still had of adoption.

One evening, when Cinnamon returned home from playing basketball with his friends, an intense discussion was going on in the living room. He saw, or rather heard, Sujit kaka. Kaka lived in a society down the road. He dropped in from time to time and Cinnamon always strategically dropped out at those times.

'Sujit, you can't generalise anything about this bakery blast last year. Investigations are still going on. Let's wait and see,' said Maa.

Kaka stabbed his index finger in the air. 'My dear Basundhara, leave aside what the media is saying. Let me tell you . . .' He suddenly spotted Cinnamon and forgot what he was dying to tell her. 'Arey, champion! Playing outside, eh? Remember me?' he inquired. Cinnamon nodded to indicate that he did, unfortunately, remember him. 'Handsome, I must say. My dear Rishikesh, you are quite lucky after all, you know. Haha!'

'Lucky?' asked Maa.

He suddenly changed the subject. 'Achha, listen, Rishikesh and Basundhara, we are going to have a very small get together at our home on the occasion of our parents' wedding anniversary, you know. Who's who of Pune will be there, you know.' He handed over an expensive looking invitation card in Marathi.

'You must come, my dear,' said Sujit.

'One of us will surely come,' reassured Maa.

'No, both of you should come. And bring along your adopted son. Don't leave him at home,' he said with a chuckle.

Baba put down his teacup and glared. Cinnamon suddenly knew what was coming. 'Sujit, would you care to repeat yourself?' he asked coldly.

'I said bring along your adopted son too,' Sujit kaka said mockingly.

'I absolutely don't appreciate your language. I must correct you. He is not our adopted son. He is our son,' Baba declared. He spoke in highly chaste Marathi which he only used when he was very angry. 'I don't wish anyone in this world to talk in that way about my son. Certainly, not in my home. Now, I think, sir, your family will be waiting, considering that you have such an important programme planned. We wouldn't want to keep you.'

Kaka smiled nervously and beat a hasty retreat. Maa accompanied him to the door. Baba picked up the card and his eyes flicked over it. 'Sujit Gawadekar,' Baba muttered. 'Insensitive donkey should be renamed Gadhavekar.' He then placed his hand on Cinnamon's shoulder and asserted, 'Cinnamon, don't let anyone ever make you feel ashamed for who you are. Be it somebody your own age or any adult. Even within our family. Nobody has that right. Nobody. Throw such people out, of your home and your life.'

Maa, who had returned, threw the invitation card in the dustbin. And that was that.

*Chapter 5*

# Rosogolla Dabba

It was the day of the history examination, the day when all the boys and girls wanted to sit next to Cinnamon. Varghese madam handed out the question papers and long answer sheets to the students. As soon as Cinnamon saw the question paper, he became slightly nervous, but it was the good nervousness which you felt when you had prepared thoroughly and just couldn't wait to start with the task. He loved history. He always felt history was about people like him and his friends, in the bygone era; real people who had fought and loved and had now passed on.

He wrote out his name confidently, with a flourish—Roshan Rishikesh Paranjape, VI-C. Very quickly, Cinnamon filled up the entire sheet. 'Extra sheet,' he requested, reddening as the entire class turned around to look at him.

Suddenly, while writing feverishly, he realised Onam Kutty, aka Raghav Menon, was throwing him the 'I-need-an-answer' look. Every time Varghese madam turned her back, Onam Kutty put his head down on his arm and mumbled something. Cinnamon strained but couldn't understand why Onam Kutty was so quiet. Of course, when you are cheating, you had to be quiet, but he was so quiet that Cinnamon couldn't hear a word and could only see his lips moving. Onam Kutty soon gave up and went on with his exam.

After the exam, Cinnamon was having a vada pav and tea at a local shop on the corner of the road, when he heard heavy footsteps which could only belong to Onam Kutty.

'Oye Roshan, happily eating vada pav? I was asking re. Couldn't you hear me?' Onam Kutty called out.

'Arey Onam, if you speak so softly, how can anyone understand?' Cinnamon responded with a counter question, his mouth half-full with vada pav. 'What question were you asking anyway?'

'What softly-softly. I asked where is Lothal and what is the name of the river in South India. I wasn't speaking that softly. It was an exam. You could hear me but still you didn't help.' Then Onam Kutty hummed the song, 'Dost Dost Na Raha.'

'Roshan, even I heard Onam,' someone said. Cinnamon turned around and was surprised to find Palli standing right behind him.

'You are supposed to be on my side,' he reminded her with a frown.

'I am on your side only. But even I was astonished how you didn't hear Onam Kutty,' she repeated.

'Yaar, I am telling you. I didn't hear. I swear. Chuck it. Have this vada pav,' said Cinnamon.

After he was done scowling, Onam Kutty had the rest of the vada pav and then parted on a sullen note, 'Check your hearing, Lambu Das.'

Cinnamon dismissed the entire episode from his mind. How could he hear a whisper?

A few weeks later, Maa said the magic words which Cinnamon always longed to hear. 'Khoka, we are going to Kolkata. Taiyyari koro (make preparations).'

It was that time of that year in Pune when you needed to wear a thin sweater early in the morning.

The entire family regularly went to either Kolkata or Ratnagiri during the week-long Christmas holidays. Maa insisted they travel at least one way by train.

The next few days went by in a whirl of examinations during the day and packing during the evening. The whole house was cleaned and locked up.

The train to Kolkata—a long blue centipede—was always in the evenings. Kolkata seemed to start from the train itself. Once the passengers had finished fighting over where to keep their bags and pregnant women and elderly persons had exchanged their upper seats for lower berths, discussions about Bengal politics and why Kolkata has the best food of any city started. Maa got very involved in such intense discussions, which went on interminably and were only broken up momentarily by hot tea and biscuits.

Cinnamon took out his box of coloured pencils and a big easel pad. He sat cross-legged on the bunk and sketched away. At important stations, where the train stopped for some time, Cinnamon stood by the train door and quickly captured some of the scenes from the stations. There was so much to capture: the hawkers shouting chai, the clean and well-kept stations, name boards on the stations, and vendors bringing in chips, water, and food. Other times, he focused on the fellow passengers and the interiors of the train. Baba and Maa had given him a set of colour pencils as a birthday gift and he wanted to make full use of it.

Travelling by train was a lesson in geography in itself and was way more interesting compared to the way the subject was taught in school. From bustling Pune to dry, hot, and dusty Badnera to the black coal heaps on dirty red goods trains in Chhattisgarh to Jharkhand's tree-covered hills and Odisha's lush green paddy fields to finally, the magnificent, monstrous, and maddening city of Kolkata.

Cinnamon felt excited when they finally got down at the historic Howrah station. After pushing through a crowd of passengers, porters, and rickshaw pullers, they piled inside a distinctive yellow Ambassador car. The car looked and felt as old as the station itself.

'Kothai jaben? (Where do you want to go?)' drawled the taxi driver, without turning around. He waited for a response while staring into the rear-view mirror.

'Khoka, tell him na,' said Baba. Cinnamon got irritated. Why did Baba forget their address every time?

'Dada, go to Raja Basant Roy Road, via Chowringhee,' Cinnamon rustled up his rusty Bengali. He rolled down the windows and beat a tune on the car door with his fingers. The sight of the glorious Howrah Bridge always took his breath away, no matter how many times he saw it. The nursery rhyme that Maa used to recite to him—'Ek Je Bagh Dora Dora Daag' (Once there was a tiger, with stripes on his back)—came back to him every time he visited Kolkata. He tried reading the wavy and colourful Bengali signboards and posters out loud, much to the taxi driver's amusement.

'We will reach in half an hour,' Maa informed didi maa on the phone. Cinnamon already knew his mother's plan of action—she would watch many Bengali plays and movies and catch up with her few friends who still lived in the city.

'By the time the trip is over, you will smell of fish and mustard oil. So, take a good bath when you return,' whispered Baba in Marathi. It was a whisper loud enough to be heard in Writer's Building or Park Street.

'Yes, Cinnamon, listen to your Baba. It's better to smell of peanuts and dried coconut powder.' Dada moshay and didi maa's home or bari was a quaint, red coloured one-storey bungalow on the main road.

As soon as they reached their destination, didi maa and dadu came out and hugged them. Baba and Cinnamon picked up the bags and took them inside. The house was spacious and comfortable but clearly, it had become too large for its inhabitants to take care of it properly.

Maa opened one of the suitcases and out popped all the goodies that she had packed for the Kolkata side of the family: spicy bakarwadi, boxes of Shrewsbury biscuits, anarse, karanji, puran poli, besan and rava ladoos, sweet round satoris, thecha, savoury chaklis, kadboli, and poha chewda. There was a black badminton equipment bag kept in a corner. Seeing the bag, Cinnamon piped up, 'Souradeep and Sudakshina have come?'

'Hain, hain. They are upstairs. Nilanjana and Tapan came this morning,' said didi maa. 'Shudokhina, Souro-esho!' They both rushed down the stairs.

'Ooooh! Bakarwadi, my favourite.' Sudakshina pounced like a tigress from the Sundarbans on the bag of bakarwadi and tore it open. Souradeep settled for the Shrewsbury biscuits.

Nilanjana maashi, Tapan kaka, and their children lived in Bengaluru. Sudakshina was a slim girl and as tall as Cinnamon. She always had her hair in a ponytail. Souradeep was of medium height and, like Sudakshina, was a school level badminton player. And though shorter than Cinnamon, he was very strong.

'Souro, arm-wrestle for the top bunk?'

'Sure!' replied Souradeep. They arm-wrestled and after a lot of effort, Cinnamon managed to win and earned the right to sleep on the top bunk bed. To sweeten the victory, there was a kol baalish at the head of the bed. He rested against it, savouring the moment.

At night, there was kumro chingri curry, rice and aloo posto for dinner. Along with it was narkel ladoos, round balls of coconut and jaggery goodness. Cinnamon had a scandalously indecent number of ladoos.

The next morning, Cinnamon observed that the domestic help, along with Nilanjana maashi and didi maa were hard at work in the kitchen, making hillocks of rosogollas, sandesh, chom choms, and langchas. Cinnamon's mouth watered just looking at the sight. There was enough syrupy rosogollas, silky smooth sandesh, golden brown chom choms, and mishti doi to feed a family of hungry elephants. And since Souro and Sudakshina were also in the house, he had to act fast. Desperate times called for desperate measures, he thought. If I don't act now, none of these goodies would be left for me. It is now or never.

That day, Cinnamon had a wonderful Kolkata darshan with Baba, his two cousins, Meshomasai, and Nilanjana maashi. Their itinerary included Science City, Dakshineshwar, Kali Bari, Victoria Memorial, the Zoo, and Park Street. Maa had gone off for a play at Nandan with her school friends.

At night, Cinnamon was tired but felt happy about visiting all the popular places in the city. He then put his plan into action.

He announced that he wouldn't eat much during dinner. It elicited the usual sighs of sympathy he had hoped for. 'Moving around in the sun all day, poor boy,' said maashi. 'Have a paracetamol.'

Cinnamon nodded and was delighted by the fact that his act was sincerely convincing.

'Headache?' asked Baba.

'No, no headache. Um . . . er . . . I mean, yes. It is . . . a little headache. I will eat a little,' Cinnamon promised. If he ate something, it would avoid suspicion.

Everyone clucked and sighed in sympathy. Only Baba raised his eyebrows. 'You had no such problem in the afternoon when you were gobbling up Mughlai parathas and chicken chops,' he quipped.

On the menu was momos, bhaat, doi maach, ghugnee, and luchis. 'How was your Kolkata darshan, Cinnamon?' asked Maa.

'It was amazing. We went to so many places. I really liked Victoria Memorial, the National Library, Science City, and, uh, Dakshineshwar Temple.' He added the temple in the end, looking at Maa, who was slightly preoccupied. She immediately brightened up as soon as she heard the mention of the temple.

'Cinnamon, I told you before also. It's not Dakshineshwar; it's Dokhineshwar. Please pronounce words correctly. I think in Maharashtra, they are not strong with pronunciations,' commented Sudakshina. Maa giggled.

'No Sudakshina. It's Dakshineshwar. Learn to read spellings in English, not only Bangla,' commented Cinnamon.

'No, it's Dokhineshwar and hello, my name is Shudhokhina, not Sudakshina.' She stuffed a big piece of maach bhaja in her mouth and swallowed it in one effortless gulp. Cinnamon watched in envy as well as disgust. She devoured the maach bhaja like a tiger devoured gazelles in the wildlife shows on TV, he thought.

'Sure Subhakshana,' Cinnamon teased. Everyone at the table snickered.

'Okay, enough, enough. Every one now focus on your food. Dinner time is for eating, not for these silly discussions,' said dadu sternly.

Cinnamon scarfed down some rice and ghugnee and then leapt onto the top of the bunk bed in the bedroom. He grabbed the kol baalish and rested his head on it. Remaining awake was the priority, so he started staring at the ceiling. His mouth was watering, thinking about all those sweets in the dabbas.

Gradually, all the sounds in the house reduced and soon, the late-night Bengali serials and political discussions could no longer be heard. It seemed like everyone had gone to bed. Now was the time!

He mustered up the courage and sat up. Gripping the bunk bed for support, he lowered himself down gingerly. He couldn't see anything at first and to his surprise, his eyes refused to adjust to the darkness. He debated for a moment whether he should stay put. But after hearing Souradeep snore, he knew it was now or never. He rubbed his eyes and decided to move ahead.

He knew that the stainless steel dabba was in the fridge. He had a good idea of where the kitchen was and how to get there from his room. Inch by inch, Cinnamon crawled from his room to the kitchen until finally, he was in front of the fridge. He opened the different dabbas and feasted on the sweets, in particular the rosogollas and chom choms. He was so engrossed with eating that he lost count of how many sweets he had eaten. Soon, his stomach reached a bursting point.

After a successful mission, Cinnamon had to make the journey back. Again, he could barely make out anything.

The blackness became a bit less intense but nonetheless, it persisted. He decided to get down on all fours and crawl across as he had before. He bumped his head against the bedroom door on his way back. He immediately bit his lips, as it was all he could do to stop himself from crying. Once in the room, he climbed up into the bunk bed very slowly.

In the morning, Cinnamon woke up to loud proclamations of 'Ki acche?' and 'Key korlo?' He tiptoed to the bedroom door and poked his head out to see what was happening. In any case, whenever Maa and maashi spoke, there was no need to strain one's ears.

'So many of the rosogollas are gone! Maago!' said Maa.

Nilanjana maashi stared deep into the tin suspiciously, as if the culprit could be found at the bottom of the jar. One by one, didi maa opened the remaining tins as well. 'Even the sandesh and chom choms!' exclaimed didi maa.

'Who can eat so much?' asked maashi with arms akimbo.

'Must be Shouro. Such a glutton he can be na,' remarked Maa. Nilanjana maashi pouted but didn't respond.

'I was sleeping really,' Souradeep insisted. Cinnamon was elated by the fact that he wasn't a suspect. He decided to nonchalantly stroll over to the sink to brush his teeth.

'Cinnamon, come here,' said Maa suddenly. He obeyed and came and stood in front of everyone proudly. 'Nilanjanadi, look at our Cinnamon,' chortled Maa. They all stared at him and started giggling. Cinnamon wondered what they were staring at.

'Khoka, I say, how many rosogollas and sandesh did you eat last night?' Maa asked very sweetly, her lips rolling every letter.

'I didn't eat any! Kubhakshana and Souradeep must have eaten them!' There were only peals of laughter in response.

'I didn't eat any,' repeated didi maa, mimicking Cinnamon.

Maa then took Cinnamon by the shoulder and dragged him to the bathroom. 'Look in the mirror baby.'

After looking at his reflection, Cinnamon felt a wave of embarrassment washing over him. His whole shirt as well as his mouth was covered with pieces of rosogolla, sandesh, and chom choms and malpua syrup stains. In his haste to get back to the bed, he had completely forgotten to even wash his mouth and hands. I look like a stupid monkey with all that sweet stuff smeared all over my face, he thought ruefully.

Soon after breakfast, Cinnamon's stomach decided it had enough of the nocturnal all-you-can-eat Bengali sweet extravaganza. He rushed to the bathroom and stayed inside for quite some time. After coming out of the bathroom, Cinnamon realised that too much of anything—even sweets—was a bad thing. But he had no regrets. Sweets were his birthright, and he would have them.

Baba smiled when he heard about the incident. 'Look at the bright side Cinnamon. Now you will know how an elephant feels when it poops,' he said, patting Cinnamon on his shoulder and embarrassing him further.

Later that evening, they all sat together for tea and chana choor. Baba wore a beautiful royal blue kurta covered in the Warli style of art with black figures. Everyone admired it and expressed many comments of appreciation. It was the first time Cinnamon had seen it. 'Baba, when did you buy this and from where?' asked Cinnamon curiously.

'Daroon! A gift from someone special, Mr Paranjape?' questioned Maa. Baba winked but didn't reply to anyone.

'Lovely kurta, Rishi. I love your taste in kurtas. Normally, you wear that dark red kurta whenever you come to Kolkata. Do you still have it?' asked Nilanjana maashi.

'Nischoy, certainly. I have both in my cupboard. The red ones are my favourites as I got them at the time of marriage. But I wear those kurtas whenever I come here, and everyone seems to think that's all I have. So, I thought, let me wear the new blue one this time for a change. It's really beautiful, you know.'

'Yes, Mr Paranjape, being with me has definitely improved your previously totally non-existent sense of style. I remember when we got married, you wore horribly coloured clothes. Good to see the change. In terms of diet, you are unfortunately still the same. No poriborton (change) of any kind,' observed Maa.

Baba and Maa always regaled everyone with stories of how they had met and what they felt. Though he had heard some of these stories before, Cinnamon loved hearing them again, as new details kept getting added.

Baba took a bite of chana choor and then remarked, 'When Basundhara came into our family, everyone—including me—liked her from day one. Our only serious doubt was: can she make polis or rotis of any kind? She had very confidently told aai that she knows. I had serious doubts as I had never seen her eating one. But I was sensible enough not to get in between a mother-in-law and a daughter-in-law.

'Then one morning Basu announced she would make rotis. She started mixing the water with the flour confidently. After a while, she kept adding more water until there was hardly any flour at all, only bits of flour floating here and there. There were no rotis to be seen, even after two hours. We were all starving and getting angrier by the minute. Finally, she cried and admitted she had no idea how rotis were made and didn't even like to eat them! Aai and aaji had to take over and rescue her.'

Cinnamon looked at Maa, who was smiling sheepishly and shaking her head. He couldn't imagine her struggling that way. Maa was so confident, so self-assured in every situation. Even his teachers were impressed and intimidated by her well-modulated voice and piercing gaze.

Maa took up the gauntlet. 'When I came to Pune, I liked so many things, especially after being in Delhi and Kolkata. But one thing shocked me, by god. Misal pav, vada pav, kanda pav, omelette pav, this pav, that pav. Also, there is dhaniya and kadi patta in everything. Ki bhoyonkor (How dreadful). Now here I am, married to a Maharashtrian. Unhappily eating non-veg once a week, like a prisoner being rewarded for good behaviour,' she lamented.

Nilanjana maashi remarked dryly, 'Well, we had found a nice Bengali boy for you. We sent you his photos also. So tall and handsome he was, I must say. Lives in London now. Became a topmost executive there. Mone ache? (Do you remember?)' asked maashi and then pinched Maa on her arm.

'Yes, I do. I even saw him on one of the business channels some time ago, if I recall correctly,' replied Maa. 'Had I married someone from Kolkata, I could have stayed closer to my culture and language.' She threw a glance in Baba's direction.

Baba snorted and shook his head. 'Whoever you might have married, I am pretty sure you would not have stayed in Kolkata anyway,' he said. He continued, unperturbed, 'Aaji had rightly warned me that if you marry a Bengali girl, be ready to eat rice and fish every day. No varan and poli bhaji. Don't complain to me later on. I told her not to worry, Basundhara is a Brahmin. But unfortunately, life, as always, had other plans for me. Now I, a person who doesn't even eat eggs, have to tolerate the smell of every meat known to mankind.'

'Only once a week, baba. I have practically become a vegetarian, you know,' Maa pointed out.

'Once a week at home. Outside is a completely different story. Can't complain to anyone also as the marriage was totally my decision in the first place,' Baba said. He looked up at the ceiling.

Tapan meshomashai made a curious coughing noise. 'Why didn't you marry a nice Marathi mulgi then? You would have got all that extremely exciting poli bhaji in the world,' said Nilanjana maashi, trying hard to prevent the smile from spreading on her face.

Baba shrugged. 'Well, aai, my baba and aaji had given me exactly the same advice. I didn't listen then. But considering my looks and sense of humour, it's too late now,' he said. Everyone, including Maa, burst into loud laughter. Cinnamon knew that he was going to cherish these moments for a long time. They were memories to treasure.

*Chapter 6*

# Tangra and Trams

Cinnamon was in a deep slumber and was dreaming about Bengali sweets and non-veg delicacies raining from the sky. He opened his mouth wide open to catch a mouth-watering chom choms but then suddenly, his dream was rudely interrupted by someone shaking him by the shoulder.

'Wake up, Cinnamon.'

That someone turned out to be Maa. He opened his eyelids enough to see the wall clock. It was 5 a.m. The sunlight was already coming in since the day started early in the east. He opened his eyes a bit wider to find that Maa was already dressed.

He groaned loudly. 'Maa, what is it?'

'Cinnamon baby, get up, get up.'

He groaned again. 'Another early morning classical music session? Diwali pahaat?'

She shook her head.

'Kakad aarti?'

中国角
চীন কোণে
包子
মোমো
春卷
স্প্রিং রোল

মশলা এবং গুল্ম
香料和香草
塔壩中國城
TANGRA CHINA TOWN
ট্যাংরা চাইনা টাউন
टेंगरा चाइना टाउन
PEOPLE OF TANGRA & K.M.C

'No re. It's a surprise, Cinnamon. Dress up. No need to take a bath, just get ready quickly. And don't forget to wear a dark shirt.' He groaned again and hoped it wasn't yet another attempt to build his character.

Cinnamon washed his face, brushed his teeth quickly, and pulled on a black polo shirt. To his surprise, everyone else was also getting ready. Even Baba had managed to get up at such an unearthly time.

Once everyone was ready, they piled in two cabs, including dadu and didi maa. Now, Cinnamon was fully awake. He couldn't restrain his curiosity anymore. 'Meshomashai, where are we going?'

'Wait and see,' he replied with a wink.

Kolkata, too, was waking up. The taxi drivers washed their cars and early morning tea vendors lit up their stoves. A few people bathed on the street. The rays of the sun streamed across, lighting up the day. The place they were going to turned out to be a congested and clogged street filled with fruit and vegetable vendors, shops of different kinds, and, most importantly, stalls of real Chinese food. Cinnamon could see that there were several Chinese people running the stalls along with several Bengalis. The range of food on offer was truly amazing: sweet rice balls studded with sesame seeds, bowls of hot clear soup with fish balls, pau stuffed with chicken or pork, crisp deep-fried pork rolls, coconut balls, homemade sausages, momos, prawn wafers, wontons . . . the list went on and on.

Cinnamon bit into a juicy pork pau—a crisp deep-fried roll—which was red from the inside. He sipped the clear chicken broth soup from a white bowl. The market, even at this early time, was abuzz with customers. Many were obviously tourists while some were locals. They had mostly come for the Chinese breakfast. It was startling to hear fluent Bengali and Hindi from a person who was Chinese. Cinnamon started taking pictures of the street and the Chinese vendors. It was so quaint to see a tiny slice of China here in Kolkata.

'Don't take so many photos of them, Cinnamon. They are not foreigners or animals at a zoo,' said Maa sternly.

'Why?'

'Would you take photos of the vendors in Shivaji market or Mandai?'

'But . . . they are Chinese.'

'They are Indians, like us. They came from China and settled in Kolkata over two hundred years ago. I myself had a few such Chinese friends in school and college days. Now, their community has dwindled a lot but they are as much Indians as you and me. If you have to take so many photos, then take some of the food.'

After a sumptuous Chinese breakfast, they went off for a Bengali movie at a multiplex. It was an action movie with an improbable storyline about a policeman going after a real estate don. The don tried kidnapping the policeman's girlfriend's sister but somehow the policemen got wind of it. There were all kinds of interludes including action sequences where the hero singlehandedly beat up many goons. The goons themselves were very considerate; even if in a big group, they always waited for the hero to finish beating one of the gang members before the next person went and attacked him. Cinnamon couldn't really follow the plot but somehow it all hung together, in a very entertainingly preposterous way.

Surprisingly, Baba, who was usually hyper-sceptical of everything, appreciated it. 'Khupach bhalo (very good). Such good acting,' he said, munching on popcorn. Cinnamon didn't understand what he liked about the movie so much.

'What did you like about the movie, Baba?'

'Everything.'

In the evening, they all went to Esplanade for shopping and ate sweets at one of Kolkata's most famous sweet shops. The shop was like a railway station practically, considering the sheer crowd of people coming in and going out. Cinnamon restrained himself to a few rosogollas this time, much to everyone's amusement.

'Khabe na? (Want more?)' Sudakshina would taunt after eating every rosogolla. 'Sure you don't want it?' Cinnamon tried kicking her but to his dismay, she always moved her legs deftly out of the way.

Soon, it was already getting dark; the sun set early in this part of the country. Cinnamon spotted one of Kolkata's ancient but cute trams and immediately suggested, 'Let's go by tram!'

'I hope you reach home before midnight,' remarked Souradeep. Cinnamon and Maa jumped into a tram that passed by and trundled along through central Calcutta. You couldn't leave Kolkata without travelling in a tram, he felt. It moved with a snail like majesty as all manner of vehicles raced contemptuously ahead of it. But he felt that it had a slow and resigned charm of its own, much like the city of Kolkata itself. When it reached the Maidan, the tram unexpectedly jolted to a stop. Cinnamon heard a short-circuiting noise and all the passengers were plunged into an all-encompassing inky blackness.

'The electricity has gone,' rang out a voice, loudly and completely unnecessarily.

Cinnamon and Maa got out of the tram and started walking. There was the sprawling and magnificent Kolkata Maidan on one side and traffic racing past on the other side. Cars whizzed by at high speed as they walked, sometimes within inches of them. The sounds were now very close: the loud blare of a bus, the whine of engine exhaust, the screech of a car braking, and the bleat of a motorcycle horn. Cinnamon felt as if he would be run over at any time. None of the taxis bothered to stop despite Maa repeatedly trying to hail them. The lights of the vehicles rushing by were merely faint commas and ellipses in the dark of the night. He clung onto Maa's hands for his dear life.

Finally, after walking for some time, they hit a traffic signal and managed to hail a taxi. A little later, as their taxi drew close to their home, he could make out things and was a tad bit relieved. When they reached home, Maa asked curiously, 'Cinnamon, were you feeling scared? You normally always pull away when I grab your hand.'

He blushed. 'No, not scared. Anyway, let it be. Don't worry.'

Cinnamon could see that Maa was not entirely convinced, but he did not want her to worry. She would then take him to the doctor, which he absolutely didn't want. At the same time, it was scary to be walking in that darkness.

## *Chapter 7*

# The Light

As always, the days flew by and before they knew it the trip to Kolkata was nearing its end. But there was one more destination to cover. They all went for a one-day trip to Santiniketan on the Bolpur Express. There they found a group of tourists from Pune and fell in with them. Cinnamon loved the sculptures and paintings and tried to listen as best as he could to the guide explaining why Rabindranath Tagore was as much a brilliant painter and visionary as a writer. 'He was a poet, a playwright, a singer, a writer, a philosopher—what could he not do? He was a polymath.'

One of the other tourists murmured, 'If the T-Rex had been discovered in Kolkata or West Bengal, it might have been called the Tagoresaurus Rex.' There was a ripple of laughter.

The guide, catching the remark, promptly said, 'Yes, Rabindranath Tagore is the only writer in India to have a dinosaur fossil named after him. It is called the Barpasaurus.' Everyone was genuinely impressed.

Maybe, one day, there would be a Roshan Paranjape Museum, thought Cinnamon. Maybe, one day, I will be really famous and have a dinosaur fossil named after me.

The next day, Cinnamon heard the words he had been dreading: 'Cinnamon, help me pack.' He ignored Maa, hoping that by doing so, he could also ignore the reality. But when he saw Baba taking the clothes out of the cupboards and Maa going off to the market, holding a long list written in Bengali, he knew it was time to go back to Pune. After all, no trip could go on forever. He realised that soon, he would be back in Pune, back to school, football, and drawing classes, back to Onam Kutty, Palli, and Mrs Kadubole.

Their bags were packed and it had all the stuff any self-respecting traveller from Kolkata would have that included homoeopathic medicines, nolen gur to make payesh and sandesh, Dhakai and Tangail sarees, cakes and pastries from New Market and the restaurants on Park Street, colourful kurtas with kantha embroidery, tins of sweet-sour aamer tock, jute items, and Bengali books and magazines. Maa often insisted Cinnamon read Bengali newspapers but he got only as far as the headlines. Their flight to Pune was in the evening, as Baba always preferred it that way. 'When you fly in the evening, you can go to sleep soon after arriving, and then wake up the next morning, fresh and rested,' he declared.

After reaching Pune, Cinnamon saw the street vendors at traffic lights selling left over red Santa caps and dresses. Huge billboards still promised a night of merriment on New Year's Eve.

Life in Pune returned to its usual routine: school, football coaching, basketball games, and drawing classes. One afternoon, Cinnamon and his buddies went for a game at a local basketball court near their home. It was a hard and competitive game and carried on till late evening.

During the game, Harpreet threw the ball to Cinnamon. He didn't see the ball and only heard it swoosh by. 'Oye Cinnamon, where are you looking?' asked Harpreet angrily. 'Didn't you see the ball?'

Cinnamon shook his head. 'No yaar.' He could have sworn that his eyes were on the ball but for some reason, he missed it when it was thrown to him.

'Where is your mind at?' said Harpreet irately.

'He must be thinking of Palli,' came the reply. They all chuckled and Cinnamon's face reddened. He did think of her often—especially during the Hindi class when Pawar madam droned on and on like a car's reverse horn—but this was certainly not one of those times. You can't daydream in a fast-moving basketball game.

Baba picked him up after the game was over. He didn't say anything initially, but while driving, he gently asked, 'What happened Cinnamon?'

'Nothing.'

'You sure?'

'Yes, nothing happened.'

'Some issue?'

'No issue.'

'Why did you miss the ball?' Baba asked finally.

'I couldn't see it,' Cinnamon said after a pause.

'Couldn't see it, in the sense?' Baba asked sceptically.

'When it is very dark . . . sometimes . . . it's difficult for me to see things,' said Cinnamon.

'How long has it been since you noticed this?' Baba asked.

Cinnamon struggled to answer. 'Since a little while,' he finally said.

Baba and Maa took Cinnamon to Dr Jayant Vichare's clinic on Bhandarkar Road, near Tilak Tank. Dr Vichare was an ophthalmologist. A forest of footwear of all sizes and colours nestled on the shoe rack outside the reception area spoke of his immense popularity, especially among the younger generation.

The receptionist smiled and motioned them to sit down. They sat underneath the framed portrait of Gondavalekar Maharaj on the wall. Baba gave Cinnamon a copy of *Champak* that he had carried with him and busied himself with *Business Standard*.

After a long wait, they were ushered into the clinic where Dr Vichare got up to welcome them. 'What a surprise to see you here, Rishikesh. You look fine though, except for your hair,' he said in a booming voice.

'I am fine. It's about my son. Cinnamon, tell Dr Vichare about your eyesight problem at night,' he said.

Cinnamon repeated what he had told Baba. 'It's like when it's dark, you can see a little, but not clearly.'

Dr Vichare carefully made notes on his notepad. 'Any other issues?'

He thought for a moment and then said, 'No, that's all.'

After some examination and further procedures, Dr Vichare diagnosed it as retinol deficiency. Maa, upon hearing that Cinnamon had retinol deficiency, took it upon herself to add lots of carrots and beta-carotene to his diet. Cinnamon suddenly found himself munching on carrots, eating lots of fish, and taking supplements.

For a while, it seemed like things took a turn for the better. Cinnamon's night vision improved and he could also attend his friends' sleepovers and play dark room. But the problem resurfaced from time to time and he struggled to describe it.

Cinnamon devised various coping mechanisms. He kept a bottle of water next to him and tasty snacks under his bed when he went off to sleep. He had memorised an exact route from his bed to the bathroom and to the light switch on the wall and knew exactly how to get there, even with the lights off. He made it a point to keep his mobile close to him, so he could switch on the torch if need be.

One day, he and Palli were cycling around in their area. They stopped at a stall for nimbu-pani and drank it from small, frosted glass bottles.

'What happens to you when it gets dark, Cinnamon?' inquired Palli.

'I can't see you right. So, it's like you are not there at all. Which is so good.'

She sighed in mock disgust. 'So stupid. Forget I asked.'

'No, wait re. When it's dark, it's like . . . sometimes I can't see that clearly. It is like being in a dark movie hall.'

'Idiot, nobody can see clearly in the dark. Everyone needs a few seconds to get adjusted to the darkness,' said Palli.

'That's not what I mean, Palli. It's like . . . for me . . . it takes a lot longer than a few seconds.'

*Chapter 8*

# A Bicycle

There it was—a carbon frame geared bike with an alloy frame. It was black, sleek, and had bright red decals.

Cinnamon feasted his eyes on this beauty through the showroom glass. Looking at it, he imagined all the rides he would have with his football and school buddies. How many questions they would have about his bike! Even his classmates who showed off their 'no filter' photos in front of international locations would have to pay attention.

'Interested?' asked the showroom assistant who had come out on the footpath. 'Want to come inside? You've been looking at it for some time.' The assistant gestured to him to come inside. Cinnamon went inside the showroom. It was one of the biggest cycle showrooms in Pune. All types of cycles for all age groups were on display. Right from small pink tricycles for girls to swanky, imported multi-geared bikes for professional cyclists, the store had it all.

He turned the price tag over—Rs 22,000. Though he knew the cycle wouldn't be cheap, he was taken aback by the price. The shop owner padded over noiselessly in his socks. He glanced at Cinnamon up and down. A smile slowly spread over his face. 'Beta, we can always give a discount. Why don't you talk to your mummy-daddy? Take my number.' He wrote his name and number on a white business card and handed it over. Cinnamon took a quick look at the name on the card—Rishab Jagtiani—before stuffing it into his wallet. 'Take a photo of the bike for your parents to see. Maybe it can be a birthday gift,' added Mr Jagtiani in Marathi. Cinnamon snapped several photos and set off.

When he got home, he showed it to Baba. 'Baba, see this cycle!'

Baba adjusted his spectacles and took a closer look. 'Are you buying it for me?' Baba asked with a straight face. 'That's very considerate. But I don't go to the office every day. So, I think you need it more.'

'Baba, I want it for my birthday.'

'I will keep it in mind. Where did you go? Jagtiani of Classic Cycles Showroom?'

'How do you know?'

'I know everything, Cinnamon. Let me see.' He clapped him on the back. 'Now let me get back to Mr Sensex and Mrs Nifty.' Cinnamon was convinced that the bike would be his very soon.

The next day at school, Cinnamon exchanged his lunch with Onam Kutty; tasty crisp appam and stew for boring palak paneer and rotis seemed like a good exchange. 'It's only namesake palak paneer,' he grumbled. Mostly palak only it is. I got so excited hearing palak paneer, but you can't see any paneer only. It's cheating yaar. You like this?'

He was surprised to see Onam Kutty relishing his palak and rotis. 'It's very tasty. Your mom cooks so well. Also, it's a break from eating rice all the time, na,' he said.

'I don't know. But anyway, guess what?'

'What?' asked Onam Kutty.

'I am getting a new bike,' Cinnamon said proudly and showed off the photos on his phone to Kutty. He felt a sense of satisfaction at seeing Kutty raise his eyebrows.

'It's a very good bike, re.'

'It's not just good, it's an amazing bike, Kutty,' Cinnamon said. Kutty chuckled in appreciation.

'Yes, re. One of our relatives in Dubai has the same bike. The point is, when do I get to sit on it?' demanded Kutty.

'You? You need to grow by at least a few inches, only then you can think about cycling. If you sit on it, your legs won't reach the pedals only.'

'Duffer, who said anything about me cycling? You will cycle. I will sit and tell you where to go,' Onam Kutty remarked, got up, and rapped Cinnamon on his head in one fluid motion.

'The bike cannot take your weight, okay. It's meant for people like me and not baby elephants.'

'Bilkul (absolutely). I am sure Pallavi is very light.'

Over the course of the next three to four months, things drastically changed at the Ghosal household. Baba and Maa were no longer eating out regularly. Delivery men from online retail portals, with their familiar brown packages, were no longer visiting their home that often. Baba himself had not gone out of Pune for a long time for his business visits. He also had become very particular about switching off the lights.

Cinnamon had a sinking feeling about where all this was going. His thirteenth birthday was approaching in June. The school year was ending and he knew he had to lock in his birthday request before the summer vacation. 'Maa, are you getting me the new bike for my thirteenth birthday?' he asked at the breakfast table.

'It will be difficult this time, Cinnamon.'

'But, Maa . . .' She looked away.

'No. I said no. You can't have a new bicycle now. We can buy a new one next year.'

'But everyone in school has a new bike.'

'This year, we can't do it. Please understand.'

A few days later, he again brought up the topic. 'Maa, why can't you get me the new bike this time?'

Maa made him sit down, ruffled his hair, and explained

gently, 'This year, we are facing many financial issues, Khoka. In our company, they are doing cost-cutting. Many employees have been laid off and our salaries have been reduced. Even your Baba hasn't been getting many projects these days. We had planned to have a vacation abroad this year, but we have cancelled it. We have loans to pay for our car and flat,' she said.

Cinnamon felt irritated. 'I want that bike,' he shouted in a shrill voice.

'No.'

'I want a new bike! I want a new bike!' He rushed across to Baba. Baba shook his head. 'You never buy me anything. This is so unfair!' he shouted and ran into his room and slammed the door.

The next day, after the school was over, Cinnamon and Palli were waiting together at the school gate for Baba to come and pick him up. Sundar, too, stood a little away, pretending to be interested in a mobile game, but was keenly listening to everything around him.

Cinnamon unburdened himself to Palli, expecting a pat on the shoulder or a joint moaning session. 'Yaar, Palli, Baba and Maa had promised to buy a bike for me. I was looking forward to it so eagerly. Now they are saying they can't buy a bike this year at all. It sucks. They had promised. I feel so terrible about it. Now, I have to wait one more year.'

Palli's response was not what he expected. 'Eh Lambu, when did they promise to buy you a bike?'

'Arey, yaar, last year re. They said, "We will see." That's as good as saying they will buy it,' he reasoned.

She shook her head. 'They never promised. You only felt they will buy it and told everyone. Parents are like that. They will say that we will do this and that but it doesn't actually happen. Till you get something, don't tell anyone about it,' she remarked.

Sundar, who had been listening to the conversation quietly, said, 'Cinnamon, your parents are not buying a new bike for you na?'

Cinnamon generally avoided any kind of interaction with Sundar, but this time he couldn't avoid replying. 'Yes. I mean no, they are not buying.'

Sundar smiled contemptuously. He pressed home the advantage. 'They won't buy such an expensive cycle for you.'

'Why won't they?'

'You are adopted na.'

Cinnamon raised his fist and came at him. Sundar backed off, aware of the power behind that fist. He went a little away and then shouted back. 'Ask them, lambu. You will come to know. You are adopted, after all. You are not their real son.'

Palli pulled Cinnamon back. 'Ignore him, that idiot.' Cinnamon shook his head angrily.

For the next few days, Sundar's words rolled around in his mind, like sand that gets stuck in your sandals at the beach in Ganpatipule. 'They didn't buy it because you are adopted.'

One evening, Cinnamon couldn't restrain himself anymore. He went to the room where Baba and Maas were sitting in companionable silence. Baba was listening to Kishori Amonkar and swaying his head while Maa was poring over a colourful Bengali literary magazine.

'Baba, when will I get a new bike?' Cinnamon asked.

Baba looked up and said in an even tone, 'Cinnamon, we have already told you that this year we cannot get a new bike. We have some financial issues this year. Next year, let's see. I promise.'

'That's not the real reason, is it?' Baba stared back. 'Because I am adopted that's why you aren't buying me a new bike. I am not your real son. That's the real reason, isn't it?' He didn't feel good saying it but it was too late, the words had left his mouth.

Maa stood open-mouthed. Even Baba was shocked. He wondered why both of them went silent. 'It's the truth! It's because I am adopted you don't buy me anything,' Cinnamon repeated. He then ran to his room and started crying into the pillow till it turned soggy. He locked the door and refused to open it for a few hours. It was only when the tears had dried up that he went and sat at his desk, blankly watching the sparrows perched on the Gulmohar tree outside. His sketchbook lay in front of him. On any other day, he would have been making sketches of the birds, but today, it remained unopened.

'If I was with my real parents, I would have got everything I wanted. They would make time for me and shower me with love and buy me a multi-speed bicycle, chocolates, clothes, and everything else that money could buy. They wouldn't scold me. They would never stop me from growing my hair long. They wouldn't make me do so many chores. And most of all, my real parents would look like me. Nobody would ever say that I look different from them . . .'

In the days that followed, Cinnamon became quiet. The fact that he was adopted played severely in his mind. I was abandoned, he thought. I don't belong to this family. They are not mine; they are strangers. My parents rejected me. I am an orphan. I was given up because something was wrong with me. My biological parents don't love me. My adoptive parents don't love me either. All such lines kept repeating in his mind.

He tried to imagine what his real parents might look like but he found only darkness. Baba and Maa also couldn't help him with this aspect as they didn't have any picture of his biological parents.

He would hear about earthquakes in Japan, tsunamis in Sri Lanka, and huge floods in Thailand. Secretly, he wished for such a thing to happen here as well. He wanted it to rain heavily so that everything would be washed away—their apartment complex with its swanky lifts, the clubhouse and the swimming pool, his school, his boring homework, his plain red cycle. And then, he wished that his real parents would appear and they would get back together and live happily ever after.

But none of his wishes came true. Their quiet lane off North Main Road in Koregaon Park in Pune neither saw an earthquake, a tsunami, nor any floods. The early morning kakas lugging grey, steel tins of milk on their motorcycles, the boisterous calls below his window by street vendors, the noisy evening bread vans—it all remained the same.

Cinnamon's teachers also noticed that he was paying less attention in class. To allay the situation, Maa started making his favourite dishes one after the other—luchis with piping hot aloo dom, gajar ka halwa with vanilla ice cream, malpua, and spicy chicken curry with basmati rice—but Cinnamon hardly touched them.

Finally, Baba asked him one morning, 'Cinnamon, would you like to talk with someone?'

'No, I don't want to talk with anyone!' he yelled at the top of his voice.

One day, in the afternoon, Cinnamon left home without informing anyone. Maa was at work while Baba was in his home office.

'Khadki Football Grounds,' he said to the auto driver. After reaching, he sat on a bench on the ground until it got dark. Luckily, none of his football buddies had come that day. He saw from a distance that some people were playing, laughing, and having fun.

I will stay here only, he thought. Then everybody at home will get desperate and call the police. They would go all crazy looking for me. He imagined TV channels and newspapers carrying elaborate stories of his disappearance. WhatsApp groups would pass on his photo and description. Twitter celebrities would tweet and retweet his disappearance until it became viral. Everyone would look for him.

Cinnamon felt as if there was no one he could call his own and his eyes filled with tears. Then suddenly, he heard a loud, rough voice. It snapped him out of his reverie. He realised that he had lost track of time and that mosquitoes were feasting on him.

'Hello, why are you still here? How many times do you want me to blow my whistle? Please get lost now or I will lock the park and go home,' someone said in Marathi.

He looked up. It was the security guard of the park, Mohite kaka.

'Oh! It's you, Roshan,' said Mohite kaka after a closer inspection. He then came and sat next to Cinnamon. 'How long have you been sitting here by yourself?' Cinnamon continued staring at the green grass and didn't say anything. His eyes were tear-laden. 'Where is your aai, who always picks you up? And what happened to your weekly football practice?' Again, there was no response from Cinnamon.

They sat like that for quite a while before Mohite kaka patted him on his back. 'Come. How long will you keep sitting here? Go home. We all have to go home,' said Mohite kaka—finally breaking the silence—in a kind voice. He hailed an auto for Cinnamon and put him in it.

When Cinnamon reached home, he saw that the light was on in their flat. He suddenly felt terrible, thinking what Baba and Maa must have gone through when he was not there. When he rang the bell, Maa rushed over and hugged him tightly. Baba did likewise.

'Cinnamon, there is someone who we want you to meet. Maa asked one day. Cinnamon shook his head. And that was that. Finally, after some days, Maa came and put her arm around his shoulder. He was sitting at his desk, sketching.

'There is someone who we want you to meet Cinnamon. You will feel better if you meet this person,' she promised him. He was initially reluctant, but then finally decided that it couldn't hurt.

Baba and Maa were delighted that Cinnamon had agreed to speak with someone. That someone was a lady, Dr Neelima Shenoy, with kind eyes and long flowing hair that reached her shoulders. She practised child psychology in a clinic on the NIBM Road and was Baba's school friend.

When Cinnamon arrived at the clinic, to his relief, there were other children of his age. The room was painted bright yellow and had plenty of soft toys. Dr Shenoy sat behind a desk and looked inquisitively at him. Cinnamon wondered what she would ask.

'What would you like to do? Would you like to play today?' Dr Shenoy asked. Cinnamon remained silent. It wasn't clear what Dr Shenoy meant when she said the word 'play'. She gave him a sheet of paper and gently said, 'You can sketch on this paper. Your Baba and aai have told me how much you love drawing. So, draw whatever you want.'

'Draw what?'

'Anything that comes to your mind.' Nothing came to his mind initially. He drew a house with a man, woman, and child standing in front of it. The boy stood well away from the man and the woman, with his hands folded across his chest. A crack ran down the middle of the house.

When the session was over, Dr Shenoy glanced at the paper and didn't say anything. 'Okay Roshan, see you in the next session.' She then shook his hand, which always made him feel like a grown-up. He was surprised by this entire interaction. There were no questions or long speeches involved.

In the second session, Dr Shenoy asked, 'What subjects do you like? What do you enjoy outside school hours?'

Not sure where this was going, Cinnamon gruffly said, 'English, history, drawing, and sports.'

'And math?'

Despite all his efforts, he couldn't restrain a smile. He immediately wiped it off his face and said, 'No, not Math!'

'Tell me about some good experiences that you have had in your life.' Why did this dame want to know about the good experiences from his life? What a lame question, he thought. 'Cinnamon, would you like to tell me about the good experiences you have had in the recent past?' Dr Shenoy repeated.

He sighed. 'Playing football and basketball with school friends. The football finals for my school. Acting in a school play.'

Next, Dr Shenoy took out two hand puppets and gave one to Cinnamon. She explained to him how he could use the puppet to say whatever came to his mind.

'Hi, I want to know why you gave me up. Why didn't you keep me?' Cinnamon said, using a bear hand puppet.

The puppet that the nurse held replied, 'We didn't want to give you up. We loved you but we couldn't take care of you at that time. There were circumstances outside our control. Please understand that we loved you.'

After the session, glasses of sugarcane juice were served to everyone. Cinnamon initially refused but then gave in. As he sipped his juice—which was very refreshing in the dry Pune summer heat—he thought about how Dr Shenoy was not too bad as compared to other grown-ups. At the very least, she listened to him without interrupting.

In the months that followed, Cinnamon visited Dr Shenoy a number of times. In each session, Dr Shenoy asked him questions but never pushed him to answer or told him what she felt about his answers. There was no prize for the right answer or punishment for the wrong one. Also, each time he was asked to draw, he drew different pictures: sometimes Baba and Maa, sometimes their home, and sometimes even the clinic. He couldn't say why, but slowly these drawings calmed him. There were other children at the clinic too, and he felt better seeing them as it made him realise that he was not alone.

There was a pretty girl with astonishingly big ears, who always sat very close to him when he drew his pictures and would stare at the drawings. She always carried a few books with her and would sometimes put her head on his shoulder sometimes. He wondered why her head was so heavy. Must be from all the studying she did, he thought. She would also occasionally burst into laughter or smile for no reason. Having her beside him was a new sensation, but Cinnamon didn't mind it. He liked her presence. Her name was Saylee and she, too, was adopted.

Slowly, Cinnamon became less depressed. Instead of the initial sense of abandonment and complete despondency, his brain now said to him, 'If I am adopted, there is nothing that I can do about it. It is neither something special nor something to be ashamed of. So many people are adopted.'

Soon, vacations were over and the school reopened. The Gulmohar, Neem, and Ashoka trees outside his apartment building began to shed all their leaves. The umbrellas, school bags, and raincoats came out and Pune's bumpy roads turned black and brown with dirty streams and rivulets. It was time to go back to school. A new academic year had started; new books, new notebooks, and all the old friends and haunts.

For Cinnamon's next birthday, though Baba and Maa didn't get any expensive gifts, they did organise a get together at home, with samosas, soft drinks, and several games including musical chairs and pass the parcel. While it wasn't like getting a new bike, it was fun.

But old feelings and questions occasionally emerged. On some days, he felt courageous and wanted to shout out, 'My name is Cinnamon! I am not only someone's son; I am a person in my own right. Look at me and not my birth certificate!' On other days, dejection struck. Who are my father and mother? Did they have dark eyes like me? Do they ever want to meet me again? But nobody ever answered these questions for him.

Sometimes, Cinnamon would imagine scenes where he was with his real parents. He wanted to know his roots. What did they look like and where were they now? Did they ever think about him? Why did they never try to contact him? What were their names?

One day, he wrote a poem in his notebook to express himself:

How I feel about my father and my mother—

As I sit here now thinking about myself,
And I don't remember doing it before,

I want to figure out so much new,
I want to know so much more.

Which one of these would my mother be?
Which one of these would my father be?
There must have been a reason
That made them do such a thing.
And when they took that decision,
How were they feeling?
Questions are so many,
And back my heart I hold,
Their eyes reflected agony,
And that's what I was told.

I know that I was lucky,
For I really had great stars,
Being born in a selfless soul,
And held in precious arms.

Sometimes it must be difficult,
For you to live behind these bars.
I wish I could make it simple,
In your every lonely hours.

I don't want to go back now,
But a glimpse of them will soothe me down,
And I'll always love you both!

Cinnamon had no clue where his biological parents were or the travails he would have to endure to see them again, but his mind was made up. He said to himself, 'If I had one wish, it would be to meet my birth parents. Just once.'

*Chapter 9*

# A Surprise

Flight no. SJ-1172 from Delhi—ARRIVED.

People were milling about in the arrival section and many were holding up boards. Cinnamon eagerly waited for Baba to come out. Baba generally rushed back from Delhi as soon as he could. This time, he had gone for well over a week. Cinnamon had tagged along for the ride to the airport.

'I think Baba has not charged his phone again,' Maa sighed, looking at her phone. Cinnamon tip-toed and looked around. There was a stream of people, all barking into their phones, but there was no sign of Baba.

Then Cinnamon spotted Baba who was wearing a thick, black sleeveless sweater. 'Baba!' he yelled. Baba waved back. He came out and hugged both of them. They walked over to the Pune airport's parking lot, where the car waited for them.

'How was your Delhi trip?' Maa asked, starting the car. 'Finally found a hotel which serves poha and upma?'

Baba smiled and said, 'No chance. Only 200 kinds of parathas, all with potatoes. The trip was fine.'

Fine? Cinnamon was dismayed. Baba normally had such entertaining descriptions of every city he went to and bought goodies from every city he visited. Baba's trips meant banana chips and vadas from Bengaluru, fried ponk and sosyo cola from Surat, bal mithai from Dehradun, and biryani and chicken samosas from Hyderabad.

When they arrived home, instead of immediately unpacking his baggage and giving him tasty tidbits and gifts, Baba had his lunch and went to the bedroom. Baba and Maa sat together in their bedroom and talked for a long time. Even during dinner, they seemed engrossed in a conversation and went back to their room soon after, which was unusual. Cinnamon decided to take matters into his own hands. He crept up to the bedroom door to investigate.

'That sounds challenging,' came Maa's voice. He pressed his ear against the door to hear Baba's answer.

'It is difficult but I am confident. At that time, in fact, I realised . . . Cinnamon!' Baba said aloud, turning around. Cinnamon burst into the room. A report lay on the desk, in front of Baba. He had his feet stretched out in front of him and a pen tucked in his ear. Maa sat on the bed. He noticed the folder and tried to grab it, but Baba took the report away.

'It's not for you, raja,' he said gently.

'Tell me what you brought from Delhi!'

'The complete collection of Sherlock Holmes and Feluda stories. I also got you biryani from Andhra Bhavan and sumptuous dalmoth from Delhi,' said Baba, his eyes twinkling.

'I want it now!'

'Maa and I have to talk about something. I will talk to you later,' Baba said firmly.

Maa ruffled Cinnamon's crinkly hair. 'You sleep now, Cinnamon.'

Left with no choice, Cinnamon sulked and exited the room as his parents continued to talk. He tried to eavesdrop but unfortunately, Maa had also lowered her voice and nothing could be heard. He eventually went to his room and fell asleep.

'Cinnamon, tell me, what do you want for your fourteenth birthday?' Baba asked Cinnamon at the breakfast table the next morning.

'Everything.

'No, seriously. Tell me what you want.'

'Maybe a bigger bicycle, which I didn't get. And also another book by Ruskin Bond or Diary of a Wimpy Kid. That's it. No, wait. Also a new pair of Nike sneakers and a cool denim jacket. That's it. Oh, and also the latest video games. That's it. And yeah, how about letting me grow my hair long? Also . . .'

His dad put up his hand, indicating Cinnamon to stop. 'You know everything is not possible.'

Cinnamon raised his eyebrows and said sheepishly, 'There is one more thing.'

'Tell me,' said Baba. But Cinnamon felt hesitant to say it.

'I won't get angry. Promise,' reassured Baba.

Cinnamon looked down at the marble floor of the living room. Trying to keep his voice steady, he said as normally as he could: 'I wanted to meet my biological parents, who gave me birth. That's it.'

His dad pursed his lips. Maa covered her mouth in shock. Cinnamon's heart leapt when he heard Baba's next words. 'Let's see what we can do.'

A few days later, Baba announced, 'Cinnamon, I am off to the adoption agency.' He was carrying a blue laptop bag.

'I want to come too.'

Baba shook his head and said firmly, 'No, Maa and I will go.' They got into the Skoda and drove off.

Later in the day, as Meena bai was pouring the evening tea, Cinnamon heard the doorbell ring. Baba and Ma entered the house. Cinnamon could make out from Maa's expression that things had not gone too well.

'Maa, did you get the information?' Cinnamon asked, half-hoping that the answer was yes.

Maa shook her head ruefully. 'Cinnamon, we are working on it.' Hearing this, Cinnamon's heart sank.

For the next few weeks, whenever the topic came up, Baba and Maa didn't say much except that they were still trying. Two weeks later, on a Sunday morning, they all sat together at their circular dining table in the kitchen. Baba had a typed sheet of paper in front of him.

'Well, Cinnamon, it was extremely difficult convincing the adoption agency to give us the information. It's something they never do. Maa and I had to really persuade them of how important it was for us. Luckily, your birth mother had given the option to contact her. Your birth father's name is Vilas Gavit and your mother's name is Aditi Gavit.' Baba paused and looked at Maa and Cinnamon to gauge their reaction before he continued, 'They both hail from Nandurbar.' Baba stopped speaking for a moment, letting the words register.

Nandurbar! Cinnamon had heard the name in one of his geography classes. At that time, it was just a word that he had to mug up and spit out in an exam. However, now, it had suddenly acquired an all-new meaning. Nandurbar was where his birth father and mother were born and lived.

After clearing his throat, Baba continued, 'The adoption agency contacted Reshama Gavali, a local businessman who is in touch with your mother. A social worker from the agency went to meet Aditi. She is still in the district but has now gone to a different village. We can meet her.'

Cinnamon's heart skipped a few beats. Maa was looking away. Baba reached across and put his hand around her shoulder, but she didn't say anything. After a while, she got up and went to the bedroom. Baba immediately got up and followed her. They were in the room until the evening. Maa didn't even come out for lunch, and only came out in the evening, had chicken soup, and then went back.

Cinnamon knew something was wrong, as Maa only had chicken soup when she was unwell. For the next few days, she came back from the office and went straight to her room. Cinnamon caught the low murmurs of conversation but couldn't actually hear anything. This continued for many days.

One Saturday morning, when Cinnamon opened his eyes, Baba stood at the bedside. 'Cinnamon, time to look up buses to Ratnapur,' he said.

*Chapter 10*

# HAPPY JOURNEY

Cinnamon searched various travel websites straight away, not believing that things were actually moving forward. He found that there was no direct train to Ratnapur town from Pune; only a private overnight sleeper bus. It had a rather suspicious name, Happy Journey Transport Ltd, and a 'prideful' feature, super luxury AC sleeper with ladies' toilet. It departed from the Sangamwadi bus depot at 10 p.m.

Cinnamon also googled about Nandurbar. He read whatever he could find about the picturesque district. It was a district on the border of Gujarat and Madhya Pradesh with a large tribal population. The majority of the people in the district were from the Adivasi community, in particular the Bhil tribe. The district had popular tourist destinations like the lush green and verdant hill station of Toranmal and the Prakasha temple. Maa will definitely make a visit there, he thought as he went through the description. Tragically, there was a major problem of malnutrition in the district, he read with sadness. Basic health, nutrition, and employment avenues were also major problems.

After all the online research, now it was now time for the most cumbersome task—packing. Normally, Maa was in charge of all the packing and made elaborate lists of items to take along, but this time she hardly paid any attention. It was left to Baba, Cinnamon, and Meena bai to pack clothes, personal belongings, and food in their big red suitcase. They also had to book the cab, clean and turn off the fridge, and tell the doodhwala, and newspaper boy not to deliver for at least two weeks.

'Two weeks?' said Cinnamon in surprise, overhearing Baba speaking on the phone. Baba scratched his earlobe.

'Should it be shorter than that?' he asked with a straight face.

'No, no,' said Cinnamon hastily and continued with his packing.

After a simple dinner of hot thalipeeth, loncha, and cold dahi, the cab was booked and they sped through the night streets to Sangamwadi, Pune's chaotic, unruly private bus stand. The massive sleeper buses, parked side by side, reminded Cinnamon of a herd of elephants, sleeping happily side by side. Happy Journey Travels bus was easy to spot at the bus stand; it was the only one that had a trilingual route board that stated 'PUNE-SURAT' in Marathi, Gujarati, and English. After paying off the taxi driver, they all climbed into their respective berths. Cinnamon had the single lower bunk while his parents had the double bunk across him.

The bus wasn't as bad as they had feared; it was actually far worse! Strange fluid stains of unknown provenance marked the bunks. The sheets looked as if they had not been changed since prehistoric times. The blankets were stinking to the high heavens. Hungry bed bugs, deprived of food, feasted on them. A strange itching sensation occurred when one laid on the back, forcing to lie face down and transfer the itch to the stomach, chest, and other unmentionable places. The AC vents blew out hot air. The charging points didn't work. Using the promised 'separate washroom for ladies and gents' required Olympic level skills in the popular Indian sport of 'hold your nose and use the smelly toilet while not falling down on moving train or bus.'

Cinnamon hit his head on the lower side of the upper bunk and rubbed his head ruefully. He always bumped his head, whether he had the middle bunk in a train or a sleeper bus. Cinnamon stretched out in his bunk; long arms and legs filled up the space as excitement and fear ran through him. Then a sudden tremor of doubt made him cold. What if his birth parents would be disappointed by him? What if his birth parents didn't feel the same way he did? What if they had nothing to say to him? He was assailed by doubts. Baba laid down and put on his jumbo earphones. Cinnamon saw him shut his eyes from time to time and sway his head, probably to Vasantrao Deshpande or Bhimsen Joshi. The space next to Baba was empty. Where had Maa gone, he wondered. He then heard a clamour nearby.

'Sir, do you care about the female passengers?' Maa asked the conductor of the bus. She stood in front of the ladies' toilet.

'Yes, maydum . . . of course maydum.'

'Have you seen the condition of this bathroom?'

The conductor mixed some chuna with gutka and threw it in his mouth. 'Maydum, it's only for one night,' he replied nervously.

'I didn't ask you whether it was for one night. I asked, have you seen it? Would you like your wife or mother to use this bathroom?' Maa yanked the bus toilet door and opened it wide. By now the women on the bus had also come forward and uttered a collective sigh of disgust. 'There is no water in the tap, the toilet hasn't been cleaned, the whole thing stinks and is unusable, and even the door doesn't lock properly,' Maa turned triumphantly to the women in the bus. 'This is their promised ladies' toilet.' She then took a snap on her cellphone. 'This will be posted to social media and WhatsApp and go totally viral,' she announced. A woman wearing a shirt with the travel company's name on it entered the bus. Maa asked categorically, 'Does any of you have any objections to the bus being delayed by 15-20 minutes while the toilet is cleaned?'

The women in the bus cried in unison, 'We will wait.'

'Yes, we will wait,' added Baba, rather redundantly. Cinnamon felt he should join in and do something heroic to add to the moment of triumph but wasn't sure about what exactly he could do. He settled for putting his hands on his waist and trying to look menacingly in the direction of the conductor. Finally, the bus was delayed by around forty minutes as the travel agency got the toilet cleaned and the water was filled in the tank. Maa stood there the whole time as did Baba.

'Aaho, you can sit down,' the employee requested in Marathi.

'I will sit down when I want to,' Maa retorted.

After the bus toilet was cleaned to everyone's satisfaction, there was a general appreciation for Maa from the women in the bus. She went back triumphantly to her bunk and laid down. Baba looked at her with undisguised appreciation.

'Mrs Ghosal, I know more than anyone else in the world that you certainly speak up for yourself, but this is the first time I have seen you speak for other people as well. You acted like a true lawyer for a change today. Well done madam! I am so proud of you.' he said with a broad smile. Maa gave her best 'I know you are' smile.

'Sir, I may not be very fluent in speaking Marathi, but I can certainly fight in that language. After all, I am married to a Maharashtrian. I have stood up for others on many occasions. You love to call me argumentative, but as I always say, don't judge anyone without a cause!'

*Chapter 11*

# Ratnapur

When Cinnamon awoke, he realised—to his delight—that it had rained heavily. A glance at his wristwatch showed it was 6:30 a.m. He pulled back the tacky, faded light blue bus curtain and looked outside. Clouds, white as sheep fleece, drifted lazily across a clear sky. The rain had soaked everything. Lush, majestic green hills rolled by and everything looked moist and shiny. Stray houses of mud and brick lay scattered on the horizon. Banana and sugarcane trees swayed in a wonderful rain-kissed breeze. Tempos rolled by from time to time, stacked to the brim with red chillies, corn, rice, and sugarcane.

The bus stopped for a break at a highway restaurant. Many people got down for a cup of tea which were served in small white paper cups. Cinnamon and Baba got down as well to have some tea. It was the typical tea from highway restaurants; nicer to smell and hold than to drink.

The men found trees and bushes in convenient locations and while looking upwards, they did what they had to do. The women stayed inside the bus. Cinnamon wondered whether nature had endowed women with bigger bladders and decided to add it to his ever-thickening 'Questions to ask later' folder.

'Baba, how much further to Ratnapur?' Cinnamon asked impatiently.

'Another two hours,' said Baba, looking at the app on his phone.

Finally, when they reached Ratnapur, it turned out to be a small, sleepy town but it had a huge concrete main road. The bus stand had a few red state transport buses parked in the front. Hawkers of fresh-green kakdi, peru, banana, and jackfruit chips energetically plied their wares.

Baba called one of them and bought some kakdi for everyone. They all munched on long strips of kakdi with salt lemon juice along with masala and chilli powder which was served on old homework sheets from school notebooks. Cinnamon felt weird, eating something without washing his mouth. Baba always shouted, 'No eating or drinking without brushing your teeth first!' Look at him now, nonchalantly eating the cucumber as if he had forgotten about his motto. Grown-ups just make up rules and then break them whenever convenient, he thought.

Cinnamon looked at the different people around him. Baba called up Reshama Gavali. 'Reshama sir, I am Rishikesh speaking. We had a safe journey and have reached the bus stand now.'

'Ya ya, come, come, Mr Paranjape. Devendra will come to pick you up in ten minutes. Stay at platform number four. He will drop you at the hotel where you can freshen up first,' squawked the voice at the other end.

Devendra turned out to be a tall and lanky man with glossy shoulder-length black hair and a thick, unruly beard and moustache which hadn't ever encountered a razor or a shaving blade. He puttered into the bus stand on an ancient looking, open-top jeep. He was wearing a dark-green kurta, hawai chappals, and faded blue jeans and had a Uni-ball pen clipped to his kurta pocket. He was the skinniest person Cinnamon had ever seen, but it wasn't the skinniness of someone who had lost weight or was weak, but rather it seemed to be his natural condition.

'Mr Paranjape?' he said in an unexpectedly rumbling, deep voice. It sounded incongruous considering his skinny frame but was compelling to listen to. It reminded Cinnamon of Irrfan Khan.

Baba shook his hands. 'Myself Devendra,' he introduced himself in Hindi. 'I will drop you at the hotel first. You can freshen up before I pick you up again.'

Baba squeezed in the front of the vehicle and Maa and Cinnamon sat at the back. Baba scanned the jeep sceptically. 'Are you sure it will get us to the hotel without falling apart?' he asked.

Devendra winked. 'Everyone asks this, and yet it hasn't broken down even once in all these years,' he said.

The vehicle sneezed and snarled before finally trundling out onto the narrow roads of Ratnapur. Cinnamon felt his heart race. This was where he was born. There were signboards in Marathi and Gujarati in shops at some places. Cinnamon spotted Bohra and Khoja businessmen in their trademark white caps manning shop counters.

'This is your palace,' Devendra said with a flourish,

pointing at the building in front. Ratnapur Palace was a four-storey white building at the end of a short driveway. The hotel was obviously recently repainted and a few vehicles, with Indian tricolours on the bonnets, were parked in the driveway. It had an attached restaurant as well, offering everything from the local Khandeshi cuisine to South Indian, Maharashtrian, and Gujarati cuisines.

The words 'Ratnapur Palace' were illuminated at the entrance. The big grey wall clocks at the reception showed the time in India and Dubai. The lobby had a stack of newspapers in English, Marathi and Gujarati. A man of medium height with neatly side-parted hair and a thick French beard greeted them genially. 'From Pune? Friends of Reshama?' he said opening up the big red hotel ledger book. 'He told me that you are coming. Myself Raju,' he said and shook everyone's hands. Raju would rub his hands and chuckle after every sentence, regardless of whether there was anything funny or not. 'Any friend of Reshama is a friend of mine.'

A porter carried their luggage to their room. Everyone was relieved that they had been given an AC room, but then Mr Raju said breezily, 'It is not working now. Anyway, at this time of the year, you don't need the AC. Let me know if you need anything extra.'

'Any non-veg options?' Baba asked, scanning the menu up and down. Cinnamon also took a look at the menu but was disappointed by the offering. It's all ghas phus, he thought.

Raju chuckled. 'Veg only.'

They unpacked and kept their clothes in the cupboard. Even though the hotel did not justify the word 'Palace' in its name, the rooms were surprisingly large and the bathrooms very clean. Thank god, thought Cinnamon when he saw the western style toilets. The room also had a large writing table, a Godrej cupboard, a dressing table with a mirror, a large attached bathroom, and a king-size bed. Most importantly, there was Wi-Fi.

'Let's freshen up. Devendra will come to pick us up in two hours. We will meet Reshama at his home,' informed Baba.

Devendra came to the hotel precisely two hours later and they set off. As they drove through a strange tangle of streets, Cinnamon saw groups of boys who had put up plastic chairs on the road and were playing cards and cricket as vehicles drove around them. 'Imagine putting up plastic chairs in SB or JM Road and playing cards!' Cinnamon chortled.

'You are welcome to try with Palli and Raghav,' Baba said with a chuckle but Maa remained silent. The jeep turned down a narrow lane with a series of bungalows. From the look of the cars parked outside, it was evident that this was a posh locality. They approached a house where a black Mahindra Scorpio was parked next to an Enfield. The Scorpio was being washed with a long green garden hose by a caretaker.

Before they could say anything, a man came out of the house. He was short, but clearly a regular at the gym. He wore a grey lungi and a white T-shirt. 'Come in, come in,' Reshama, their contact in Ratnapur, said warmly and then opened the front door of the car where Baba was sitting. He shouted something at a young girl standing at the entrance of the door. She ran inside after hearing the words. Cinnamon guessed that it would be to prepare something to eat for the guests. The house was dark when they entered inside. The living room was plush with a flat-screen TV, two navy blue sofas, a Kashmiri carpet, and a low chandelier.

'There is no power right now. It goes off for a few hours from time to time. No telling when it will go, when it will come,' Reshama said half-heartedly.

'Could you please open the windows?' Maa asked politely. The servant, who was serving them tea and snacks, opened the two big windows, allowing sunlight to stream into the living room.

'Devendra told me about you,' the man said in Hindi pointing to the lanky fellow who had come to the bus station to pick them up. 'He came to know about your issue and in turn, he asked me whether I could help. He knows that I am from that same village. I know countless people there. I know this area very well, very well,' he said. 'Like the back of my hand. Be it in the gram panchayats or police or local bureaucracy.'

A young girl walked in after a while and served paatre, sev bhaji, phalari chewda, upma with plenty of green peas, and hot tea. The food was served on stainless steel plates covered with dull green banana leaves. Cinnamon could tell from Baba's slurps that the tea had satisfied him. Only Maa didn't have much of an appetite.

Reshama looked at Devendra and recalled something. He said, 'It took me a while because she changed her name after her second marriage and now lives in a different village. I knew her father and mother too. She went to Pune for some time and worked there but came back.'

'Why did she come back?' Cinnamon interrupted.

'People here are like that only. Though they may go away for better prospects, they still want to come back. Their hearts are here after all, in this beautiful place.' Reshama paused a little and took a sip of the tea but his eyes didn't leave the three people in front of him. Then looking keenly at Cinnamon, he said, 'Devendra asked me if I knew any Vilas and Aditi Gavit from Moregaon village of Ratnapur taluka who went to Pune and stayed for several years there. It took me some time to work it out. I believe now she lives in a village in the hills. She and her husband run a small hotel. I met both of them recently.'

'How are you so sure that they are the same Vilas and Aditi?' Cinnamon's father asked. He had come so far and yet a small part of him was still unsure. 'If it is not them then it will turn out to be a wild goose chase for us.'

'Don't worry. It won't be so. I have already found out about her,' Reshama said curtly, with the tone of a person who dislikes being questioned. 'I told you that in that particular village where she hailed from, she had married a boy from a different community and gave up a child for adoption when she went to Pune years ago. She did so because of economic reasons.' Cinnamon saw Baba nod and lean back on his seat. He was a little reassured after hearing this. 'Moreover, I am from the same village. I know her and her parents as well.'

Cinnamon was lost in his thoughts and barely heard Reshama's words. He had always wondered who his birth father and mother were, and where they were. He couldn't fathom that he was on the verge of meeting them. What would their reaction be when they see him? How would they feel to see him after so many years? Would they ask him to stay with them? For the first time, he felt nervous.

'Can't we go today itself?' asked Cinnamon, unable to control the question that was on top of his mind. Reshama shook his head but not unkindly. Maa had kept her plate on the table, with the upma half-eaten, and was half-heartedly sipping the tea. Baba urged her once to eat more but she shook her head.

'What do people from here do for employment?' asked Baba.

'If they have land, they work on their small plots. Mainly harvesting sugarcane in Bardoli and Junagadh in Gujarat during the season. Educated youth are now heading to Mumbai, Nashik, and Pune.' He then added with a laugh, 'Practically speaking, the whole of India is in Mumbai and Pune.'

The conversation was broken when Devendra came back into the room. 'This is my colleague, Devendra. He has come here as a part of a . . . a . . .' Reshama searched for words.

Devendra waited for a few seconds before adding, 'Fellowship.'

'Yes, that's it, a fellowship!' Reshama agreed. He then explained the plan of action. 'Tomorrow, I am busy with some official work but Devendra will help you. Devendra, tomorrow morning, please take them to the village to meet Aditi Gavit,' Reshama instructed. 'Right now, take them back to the Hotel Ratnapur Palace. It's an A-class hotel. Best hotel in Ratnapur,' he added.

'I have heard of three-star and five-star hotels . . . but what is A-class.' The question erupted out of Cinnamon's mouth.

As both Reshama and Devendra stared at Cinnamon, Baba cleared his throat and whispered in Cinnamon's ears, 'If you get clean towels and running water and don't get eaten up by rats or bitten by mosquitos, then you are at an A-Class hotel. And now no more questions please.' Then, Baba looked at Reshama and said, 'We have already checked in at the hotel. It's a very nice hotel. How long will it take us to get there?'

Reshama misunderstood. 'Hardly five or ten minutes.' He waved his hands dismissively to show how little time it would take.

'No, I mean to the place where Aditi is. How do we reach the village?'

'Oh! It will take you around thirty minutes or maybe

one hour to reach. It is better that you leave early in the morning. You have come at the right time to this area, in this month of July. Everything will be lush green and beautiful with the monsoon rains. The natural beauty is breathtaking,' Reshama exclaimed.

The fan started whirling above and the red light on the TV turned on. Reshama casually asked, 'Will you have lunch here?' He reached for the remote and called the serving girl.

'Say yes, Baba!' whispered Cinnamon as he smelled something delicious. He looked forward to eating the local delicacies from his birthplace. But his hopes were dashed. Maa and Baba exchanged a glance—which was always a bad sign—and Baba got up.

'Thank you so much for all your efforts. It would never have been possible without you. We are really grateful. However, I think it would be good if we get going now. We thank you for your time and support,' Baba informed Reshama.

After saying their goodbyes, Baba, Maa, and Cinnamon along with Devendra got in the jeep and headed to the hotel. 'You must ask the hotel to make you khandesh style masoor dal khichadi or kadhi khichadi. In this Khandesh region, khichadi for dinner is a speciality. Have it with ghee, buttermilk, and achaar. Ultimate comfort food,' said Devendra to distract everyone from the wheezing noise of the jeep.

Baba nodded in acknowledgement. 'Did you notice how quickly they served us food? I always like good home-cooked food, especially after a long journey,' said Baba appreciatively.

'What good home-cooked food? Must have bought it from some nearby restaurant and heated it up,' snapped Maa. 'Nobody puts so much garam masala at home.'

Catching Devendra's impish smile in the rear-view mirror, Cinnamon guessed that Maa was right.

'Whatever it was, it was very tasty. No doubt,' observed Baba.

'And what about employing someone so young! It is against the law; no doubt about that either,' Maa retorted again. 'I hope we at least have a pleasant experience in the hotel,' she added.

'It is a good hotel, aunty. I have stayed there. Whoever comes through Reshama sir, stays there only,' said Devendra reassuringly.

'Don't call me aunty!' exclaimed Maa as some of her old bounce returned. Cinnamon felt glad that his mother hadn't lost her spirit completely. Nobody said anything after that.

After reaching the hotel, Baba and Maa changed their clothes and slept off quickly. Cinnamon couldn't sleep so easily. This was his city. He was finally here. He wished to run away and go to meet his birth father and mother on his own. But he knew that wasn't possible and he would have to wait.

In the night, Cinnamon, Baba, and Maa went for a long walk around the small town. They saw young boys on huge, expensive motorcycles whizzing down the roads and roadside stalls with large white flare lights selling khichadi, pav bhaji, fried rice, spicy pulao, and 'Chinese noodals'. They stopped at the Jai Maharashtra Schezwan Chinese Noodal Centre and had khichadi while standing. Maa also had chicken noodles. Cinnamon got goosebumps when he saw his own features in so many faces around him. He also realised, from all the conversations around him, that there was a babel of tongues. Every time he spoke to a vendor, he got a reply in a different language that included Bhili, Pawari, Mauchi, Kokni, along with Marathi, Hindi, and Gujarati.

He then overheard somebody telling a vendor that Ratnapur was a town where 'important things' happened. He chortled a little. 'This is such a small place, Maa. Imagine living here?' Cinnamon said.

Maa looked at him with her head cocked. Baba gulped down some of his khichadi and smiled but didn't say anything.

'Khoka, do you think it would be very different from living in Pune?' asked Maa.

'Of course! It would be so much different. You would probably end up saying "Hi" to the same person twenty times in a day,' replied Cinnamon.

'Cinnamon, when I was your age and even older, I dreamt of travelling to and living in different cities in India and abroad. The idea sounded so glamorous. So, as a child, I loved visiting our relatives in Delhi and Hyderabad. I went to Pune for my college education and worked in Bangalore. I did my master's in the USA. I certainly enjoyed all the freedom I got and the crazy, wonderful experiences. But there is something I read in a book once, which I eventually realised is true: Over time, whoever you are and wherever you live, you end up with a small group of people anyway, which is similar to living in a small village. Your friends, family, your husband or wife, office colleagues, college and schoolmates, your neighbours, people you meet on your commute—that's everyone's village. If you have these good people around you, isn't that all you really need in life?'

Cinnamon disagreed but didn't want to express it at that moment. They walked back to the hotel in companionable silence. He grabbed her hand. Maa softly sang one of her favourite Bengali songs to herself which she usually sang when she was deep in thought. Cinnamon knew it very well. He even knew some of the opening lines by heart.

The song was 'Purano Sei Diner Kotha.'

*Chapter 12*

# Up the Hill

After a quick breakfast of crisp green methi dhapate with chutney and sugar and some tea, they set off with Devendra who came precisely at 7:30 a.m. As the town was small and since there was no traffic during such early hours, they were out of the town in no time. Soon, they got off the highway and onto the village roads. The jeep juddered up and down and the distances between the houses grew as they made their way to their destination. Cinnamon noticed that the houses were generally of brick and mud with tiled and sloped roofs. Though the road at times deteriorated very significantly, it never totally disappeared and even when they went deeper into the countryside, electricity poles and mobile towers kept them company.

Occasionally, groups of young boys stopped the jeep using a long, thin tree branch across the road. 'Oye paaji, dus rupaiya,' called out one of them to Devendra in Hindi. The boys were short and skinny and their words and manner were playful but there was a touch of menace underneath all that play, felt Cinnamon. Devendra shook his head but Cinnamon noticed that he didn't drive straight through but instead always cajoled the boys into giving way. This happened several times. On one occasion, Devendra did indeed hand out a ten-rupee note.

'Do they ask everybody driving down this road for money?' enquired Baba.

'I know some of them,' Devendra said. 'This is a popular pastime among the kids here. It's nothing to be alarmed about. You can ignore it too. But you have to be careful not to pay too often, as they can start demanding even more,' he asserted. 'You can think of it as a highway toll,' he added teasingly.

Maa spoke up, 'If this road is a highway, young man, then my home is the Rashtrapati Bhavan!' For the first time Cinnamon saw Maa smile since they had decided to go to Nandurbar, but it disappeared quickly. He also noticed that Maa was wearing black shades, something she rarely did.

'I spoke to your mother. She wants to meet you at the eatery that they run,' informed Devendra. It took some time for Cinnamon to realise that Devendra was speaking to him. He was startled to hear him refer to another lady as his mother. He then wondered why Devendra didn't mention his father but he let it be.

Cinnamon became sightly nervous realising that the decisive moment was coming closer. What would he call his birth mother? What would she feel when she saw him? All these thoughts started repeating in his head again.

'How much longer?' asked Baba with no emotion in his voice.

'Five minutes, sir,' replied Devendra and sure enough, a few minutes later, he stopped the jeep in front of a shack. Cinnamon saw the board on the top of the shack which read 'Ganesh Hotel and Restaurant' in Marathi. He also observed that it was like any other roadside shack with some plastic chairs and a grey tin roof to keep one warm in the rains and cool in the summer. It also had bedsheets hanging from one corner to keep the rain out. Obviously, no card payment facility would be possible at such a place.

'Wait a moment,' said Devendra, jumping out of the jeep. For a few minutes—which felt an eternity to Cinnamon—Devendra Singh was inside the shack. Then Cinnamon saw a woman come out with him. His heart jumped with joy, anticipation, and nervousness. Her hair was oiled and tied back and her lips held a smile. The hardships of her life were etched in every wrinkle on her face and the sagging skin near her chin.

I have waited for this moment for so many years, Cinnamon thought. This is her. This is the lady who gave birth to me. My mother!

He stood at one place looking at her. His eyes were teary. The woman then came and stood in front of him. She wiped her tears with the end of her lugada sari and glanced at Baba and Maa who stood at a distance. And then Cinnamon was enveloped by a warm embrace that he had never felt in his life.

Why did you give me up? His heart screamed but no words came out of his mouth. And where is my father?

It was only when Baba and Maa came closer that they released each other. Wiping her tears, Cinnamon's birth mother invited them inside the restaurant. Once inside, she introduced her husband to everyone. Cinnamon saw that his birth mother's husband was a short man who was dressed in a spotless white kurta and a clean dhoti. He did namaskar to them but kept away politely. It was only after they all had sat down around a cheap white plastic table and the tea had been served with some pakoras did Aditi Gavit finally began narrating her story.

'I was in a relationship with a boy from a different community. Initially, there was opposition from both our parents but we finally convinced them. We got married in a simple ceremony,' she said. 'We had two children here. Later, we decided to migrate to Pune for better opportunities. Both of us were so young.'

Cinnamon looked back at her. She was beautiful and her face was so expressive. It resonated a myriad of emotions. Cinnamon also noticed that her Marathi was so different from what he was used to hearing in Pune; it was rich, colourful, and very rustic in its vocabulary and accent.

'I worked as a domestic servant and my husband worked at various odd jobs,' Aditi continued. 'We were in Pune for four years. After two years in Pune, we had a third child—you,' she said, pointing at Cinnamon. 'But then tragically, in a collision with a tempo, my husband died. We rushed him to the hospital. By that time, it was too late. For a year, I somehow tried to manage, but it was not enough. Taking care of three children on the money I earned as a domestic servant was becoming impossible for me.

'I then came to know about an agency in Pune and they promised me that the child would be well-educated and taken care of if I surrendered the child. At least one child, they pointed out to me, could get a chance for a better life. After a lot of discussions and with a heavy heart, I went ahead and gave him, thinking I could meet him again later. I even specifically put it in the records that the boy should be able to contact me if he chose to.'

From time to time, customers would stop by but they were handled efficiently by her husband. A Marathi Kalnirnay calendar and two framed photos, with faded flower garlands, hung from the wall. Aditi got up from her seat and came and sat beside Cinnamon. Her hands gently caressed his head. Cinnamon kept his head bent low.

'A few months after I had given him up, I went back to the agency. All they said was that as per the document that I had signed, I had given away all rights to the child. I was told that it was best for the child that I should not enquire, and till the child turned eighteen, nobody would contact me. Even my husband had died. I felt so alone ...' She stopped speaking as her throat choked with sadness and grief. Not being able to control herself anymore, she covered her face and wept. Cinnamon's eyes also started welling up.

After a few minutes, amidst sniffles, she began speaking again, 'I consoled myself that the child would be living a good life somewhere. For several years, I somehow carried on in Pune. Finally, I decided to come back here with my two children. I then had to make a fresh start. What option did I have? My parents eventually arranged my marriage with him. His name is Santosh.' She looked at her husband and managed a smile. 'Together, we started this hotel. The highway had been newly constructed then. So many vehicles used it. It proved to be a good opportunity for us. People use this road to go to the top of this hill here.'

'But . . . why did . . . you . . . let . . . me go?' Cinnamon said, crying profusely. Aditi simply shook her head and said nothing. Cinnamon asked his next question, as if he had not heard her speak, 'Did you never think about me?'

Aditi took out a box and from it, pulled out woollen baby clothes and a small old rattle, wrapped lovingly in old, crumpled Marathi newspapers. 'These are yours. I kept these with me. This was all that I had of you. I used to look at these and cry. I thought of you every day,' she said wistfully.

'I never forgot about my son but sometimes, life takes its own course and we as human beings have to accept it. There were moments when I thought about looking for you but there was no way of finding out where you went. Imagine my shock when a month ago, Reshama saheb called me and said that my son wanted to meet us. I thought he must be joking. Little did I know that my dream was about to come true and in the most unexpected way.' She took a small pause to wipe the tears from her eyes. 'And look at you now. You have become a smart and confident boy. I feel so proud.'

'What about my father? What did he look like?' Cinnamon asked. Aditi took out several photos, including a big framed photograph. The name was neatly written in Marathi below the photograph: Vilas Krishnarao Gavit. Cinnamon could definitely see a resemblance; the same strong face, long sharp nose, dark skin, crinkly hair, high cheekbones, and a curious, mischievous look in the eyes.

As if reading his mind, Aditi chimed in, 'You look a lot like him. He was also very tall.'

Cinnamon suddenly realised that these photos were all that he would ever have of his father. His eyes welled up with tears. 'What was he like as a person?' he asked between sobs.

Aditi dabbed his eyes with the end of her pallu. 'He was very popular and could mix with anyone. In every function, he would always take initiative and be at the forefront of organising get-togethers and activities of different kinds. He loved singing folksongs and powada. People would always ask him to sing and play the dhol tasha. Whenever you saw him, there would be at least a few people around.'

Cinnamon began to play with the crumbs of the pakoras that lay on his plate. Santosh politely intervened and said, 'I think it's better all of you have lunch.' Everyone agreed. Soon, papad, dal, makka bhakri, and vangi bhaji were served. Cinnamon noticed that the adults were trying to hold a conversation. They spoke of village politics, of life in the city, and even of the weather.

'Will you be here for many days?' asked Aditi, her voice trembling a little.

'We are here for at least two weeks,' reassured Baba. 'We both have taken a leave. I am anyway self-employed.'

She brightened up, hearing these words, and then continued to tell her story. 'One of my employers encouraged me to study further. I had otherwise given up after a certain age. I used to do the domestic chores during the day and then study afterwards. It was the madam of the house, who gave me the used books of her children,' she said proudly. 'They both went to the US later on.'

Looking out of the shack, Cinnamon saw that the sun had begun its descent for the day. That's when he heard Baba asking him something. 'Do you want to stay?' Cinnamon stared at Baba. He repeated the question. 'Do you want to stay here tonight, Cinnamon?'

He saw his birth mother nodding her head and smiling. 'That would be nice. In fact, you all can come to my house. My other two children have gone to Nandurbar town to stay with my sister's family.' Cinnamon heart's leapt.

'Devendra, what will you do?' Baba threw the question to him. Devendra had been sitting at a respectful distance.

'I will drop you and then go back home.'

'Won't it get late?' Maa asked again. 'Will it be safe?'

Devendra shook his head and said, 'I can manage.'

The matter was settled. The four got into the jeep again. Santosh started his motorcycle and Aditi sat sideways behind him. Soon, the jeep began its journey down a slope towards Aditi's home. Cinnamon felt the wind blowing on his face; fresh and innocent wind that seemed to be untouched by pollution of any kind. Within a few minutes, or so it felt, they reached Aditi and Santosh's home, inside the village.

It was a simple pucca house with a granite floor and a sloping, tiled roof. There was a sitting room, a room where Aditi and Santosh slept, and another room for the children. Two portraits hung on the wall and were covered with faded marigolds. An old TV set and a sofa were the main pieces of furniture. Cinnamon, Baba, and Maa stretched out on the floor on a simple satranji. Baba and Maa fell asleep immediately but Cinnamon kept tossing and turning. It finally dawned on him—he was at home. But for now, he still felt like an outsider.

## *Chapter 13*

# The Bathroom Outside

'Remember not to put soap on your face and eyes before you pick up the lota. Also, don't let the lota go into the bucket,' cautioned Aditi, who had woken up before everyone else, bathed, and was cooking breakfast. Santosh made the tea for everyone.

Cinnamon and his parents bathed in the bathroom outside. Cinnamon was not at all used to the Indian style squat toilet. It required quite an acrobatic effort to squat, do his business, and get up again. Two years ago, his school team had gone to Aurangabad for a football tournament and they had stayed in a hostel. There was only one western-style bathroom there and thus, there was a lot of demand for it. He studiously avoided the squat toilet there, even though it meant waking up before everyone else.

'Baba, the bathroom is outside the house,' he said, giggling. The only other place he had come across a similar scenario was at ajoba and aaji's home in Ratnagiri.

'Even in Pune, Cinnamon, if you go to old wadas, the bathroom is outside the house. Rujuta Diwekar has said that in the past, people used to only eat at home and go out to use the bathroom. Now it's the reverse,' Baba said.

'That's why all your city folks have so many health problems,' declared Aditi. 'To stay alive, you keep popping one pill after the other. One to sleep and one to get up, one to become hungry and one to digest the food, and then another one to get the food out,' she scoffed and then went inside to get the breakfast. Everyone's tummies were rumbling.

The breakfast consisted of piping hot makka bhakri, loncha, onions, and thecha with curd served on big stainless-steel plates. They sat on the floor to eat the hearty breakfast and finished it with a generous cup of hot tea.

Seeing Cinnamon's moist eyes—courtesy of the spicy food—Aditi gave him, as well as Baba, a fistful of sugar on the plate. To Maa, she gave a banana. 'Don't drink so much water!' she chided them in her colourful village Marathi. 'Water doesn't help in reducing spiciness. Eat sugar, banana, or curd.' Aditi couldn't control her laughter as she watched the three city-slickers unable to eat the spicy village food.

Cinnamon smiled wanly. Baba quipped, 'You know we are all from Pune, but you still prepared such spicy food! Have mercy on us please!'

Cinnamon focused on the comforting white curd and sugar and pushed away the spicy thecha to a corner of his plate, where it sat and taunted him.

'My boy, you are from Nandurbar but you speak and eat like a true Punekar,' said Aditi.

After breakfast, Cinnamon took out the gifts he had brought from Pune: gold bangles, a Paithani sari, and earrings. Aditi then brought a plastic bag that had some gifts in it and presented it to Cinnamon. 'I got you something too,' she said excitedly. She had bought a silver locket that had a Ganesh picture and some T-shirts and jeans.

'You need not have bought all this,' said Maa.

Aditi turned and looked fixedly. 'I can buy whatever I want,' she said assertively.

Cinnamon went for walk around the village with Aditi as he wanted to see everything. They said very little to each other. It was so fresh, green, and breathtakingly beautiful during the monsoon time. Cinnamon took in all the beautiful sceneries. They came across a stream, where Aditi scooped up some water and drank it. 'This is from the mountain top and is very clean,' she assured him, feeling amused by the expression on his face. Feeling self-conscious and remembering his mother's stark warning, 'Be careful about the water,' Cinnamon initially hesitated but then scooped up water in both his hands and drank it gingerly. After a few sips, he threw all caution to the wind and started gulping it down.

'Is it safe?' he asked after drinking it.

She smiled and ruffled his hair. As if reading his mind, his birth mother giggled and said, 'I know your Maa will tell you never to drink water here and there. Don't worry, nothing will happen.'

As they walked together, Cinnamon keenly observed all the surrounding area. He noticed that the main crop in the village was rice. The tall, green swaying paddy stalks were visible everywhere. There were huge fields used for harvesting. He then came across a bunch of local kids; the boys were playing kho-kho, hide-and-seek, and cricket, while girls were playing hopscotch. Sitaphal, bora, and bananas trees were visible everywhere. The women in the village wore silver jewellery; it was a regular practice in these parts.

'What was my birth father like as a person?' he asked, while they walked.

'He was so dashing and handsome. Everyone liked him. Though there was opposition from both our parents, he managed to eventually convince everyone. He had a very caring and warm nature.'

'What kind of food did he like to eat?'

'He liked spicy food of course. In particular, dhapate, dhirde, lasun chutney, patoda, and thecha were his . . . our favourites.'

'Was he good at drawing?'

She looked at Cinnamon with a warm smile. 'No. He was good at singing and dancing. He loved to sing Rodali songs of our community. These songs are about every aspect of life. He also danced in our tribal dance troupes. I remember he had once even gone all the way to Mumbai to perform at some dance festival there.'

'How did you meet him?'

'He was in our village only but we were too shy to speak to each other. There is a village bazaar that happens every year during the time of Holi. So many people come there from Nandurbar and even other states and districts. It's a full dhamaal. Many marriages are fixed there only. So was ours,' she said, blushing. 'In our culture, the groom's side has to pay dowry to the bride's side. Of course, the demands have to be kept reasonable,' she explained.

'Was my father good at math?'

'I am not sure. Are you?'

He looked down at the ground. 'What about my brother and sister? What do they do?' Cinnamon asked, ignoring the question that was posed to him.

'Your sister studies in the local government school here. She is in the eighth standard. Your brother is in the eleventh standard. He now stays in Nandurbar, in a hostel for tribal students. He has got a scholarship,' she said.

'Can I see their photos? I would also like to meet them.'

After a pause, she said, 'Yes of course you can meet them. I will show you their photos when we go back.'

When they returned home, she showed him the two buffaloes they had near their house. She sat on a stool and started milking them. Fascinated, Cinnamon pleaded, 'Let me do it, please.'

'Do you want to kill the poor animal?'

'No, let me try.' He took the teats and tried squeezing them. The buffalo immediately let out a groan of protest.

Aditi guided him and finally, some milk did fall in the steel grey bucket. Aditi clapped in appreciation.

'Not bad for the first time. But it takes time. Now let me take over.' She skillfully milked the buffalo till the bucket was full to the brim. It was rich and foamy on the top. 'We consume this milk at home mostly. We don't sell it,' she said.

After the milking session was over, they went back to the home. Baba and Maa had brought with them photo albums as well as a notebook that recorded the different milestones: the age at which Cinnamon spoke his first word, when he started walking, when he said his first complete sentence, when he started attending school, etc. Cinnamon also showed Aditi his book of sketches.

'These are so beautiful. Khup chhaan (very good),' she said, going through them.

'Cinnamon loves sketching. He first started doing it on the walls of our home. We had to spend a lot of time erasing all his drawings before we vacated the flat,' said Baba and chortled. He showed her photos of the drawings Cinnamon had made on the walls of their old flat in Model Colony.

'What kind of drawings are these?' asked Aditi.

'It's modern art,' said Baba, guffawing. 'And every time we asked him that who made all these drawing, he would say that 'Nahsor' did it and not Roshan. And when asked that why doesn't he use drawing paper, he would very seriously say, "The walls are my big drawing paper."'

'Your landlord was really nice, eh. They said nothing about him drawing on the walls?' asked Aditi. Maa tossed her hair back and laughed. It was the full-throated laughter that Cinnamon had not seen or heard in a long time. Baba smirked.

'Laugh away, madam. When Mr Mane saw those paintings, I don't remember you laughing. He had some very interesting things to say about it,' remarked Baba.

Baba said, 'I remember Cinnamon liked dropping things from the balcony. He dropped toy cars, my wallet, glasses, plates, notebooks . . . basically anything and everything you can think of. He would also pull clothes off the line and throw them downstairs. One day, he dropped my briefcase from our flat on the fourth floor. By God's grace, it did not hit anyone but instead fell on somebody's car roof! I had some explaining to do that day.'

'This is Cinnamon's photo when he had come home for the first time,' Maa pointed out. 'This is a photo of his first birthday. And this is a photo of him on his first day at school.' Baba had downloaded videos of Cinnamon's early childhood on his mobile and showed them to Aditi. They had also brought along photos and videos of his football exploits.

'This is the photo of him saving the goal during his school football finals,' Maa pointed out.

Aditi looked at it for a long time. 'He is the goalkeeper?'

'Yes.'

Later, Aditi proudly showcased the photos of her son and daughter on her phone. 'I am not very comfortable with this phone,' she said apologetically.

Cinnamon stared at pictures of his siblings. 'They look so different,' said Cinnamon in surprise and amusement.

'Maharaj, there is no such rule that children have to look exactly like their parents,' said Baba. 'Anyway, let's help with the lunch,' he added, a little too quickly.

The lunch consisted of bharli vangi, a crushed onion with a dash of salt, a slice of lemon, achaar, and cucumber slices. In the corner of the house, Cinnamon spotted some green-yellow fruits that were piled up in a stack. They were round in shape and looked similar to a lemon. He had never seen it before. 'What are these?' he asked.

'These are the Mahua flowers. We use the sap of the flowers and make a drink out of it. The locals sell the drink especially during the winter and monsoon seasons,' responded Aditi.

'Wow, so you can pluck flowers from any tree and nobody minds?'

She said, in a chiding tone, 'You think we are city people or what? The ownership of specific trees is passed from one generation to the next. So, each family has rights to their own lot of trees.'

Cinnamon asked mischievously 'Can I have it?'

'No, it is not for kids. When you become big, then you can have it,' replied Aditi. When would I become 'big'? Cinnamon thought. Am I not big enough already?

The day passed peacefully and Cinnamon moved around the village, taking in all the sights and sounds. He saw how simple everything was and wondered what it would been like to grow up in such a village, to go to school here, and live here.

At night, they had a meal of rice and chicken. 'In this area, non-veg is a must. Be it fish, chicken, or for the few who can afford it, even mutton occasionally,' Aditi declared.

'I can see that in this aspect, Cinnamon is truly his mother's son, from both sides,' Baba replied.

Aditi grinned. 'Why do you call him Cinnamon? What does the word mean?'

'Cinnamon is the English word for dalchini. When he was small, he couldn't pronounce the word Cinnamon and for a long time, he called himself Cimmanum or Cinnamum—a real tongue twister. We found it so cute that it became his nickname,' Baba said.

Then Maa added with a giggle, 'He hates it now though.'

## Chapter 14

# Misal Pav

The next morning, after a quick breakfast of tea, dhapate and nistyachi chutney, Cinnamon decided to tag along with his birth mother to the restaurant. Both of them squeezed along with Santosh on his motorcycle. Cinnamon let his long legs dangle out, enjoying a freedom he couldn't dream of in Pune's traffic.

At the restaurant, Aditi picked up a broom and swept everything and then put fresh marigolds on the framed photographs of her parents.

'Can I help you?' Cinnamon asked.

She handed him a yellow wet mat. 'You can clean the tables with this.' Cinnamon did the task assigned to him enthusiastically. Santosh took out the cash register and counted the notes. Aditi efficiently cut up small hills of onions, tomatoes, carrots, and other vegetables. One employee prepared the huge black-grey degchi of tea; it would boil and bubble the whole day.

There was no menu as such. People came in and asked, 'What's there to eat?' Aditi rattled off without any hesitation, 'Piping hot poha, samosas, bhajis, and dhirde.'

'What else?'

'Upma, methi dhapate, and chutney.'

'You don't tell them all in one go?' Cinnamon put his query to her.

'Never give too many options, my boy. It confuses people.' She then turned around and yelled at the employee. 'Oooo! What the hell are you looking at on your phone? When are you going to give us the dhapate? After we die?' The man, who was flicking through his mobile, got embarrassed and speeded up things.

Cinnamon studied every customer, trying hard to draw conclusions about them the way Sherlock Holmes did. Suddenly, a white Mahindra Scorpio halted a little bit away from the restaurant. Four men got out from it.

'Maushi, four plates of missal pav and four chai, double quick,' a man called out in a smooth voice. He wore a neat, crisp black button-down shirt, blue jeans, stylish brown shoes, and a belt. Shades and a thick gold watch completed his stylish look. Cinnamon initially thought the men were quite old but after they came closer, he realised that three of them looked only a few years older to him. Aditi cleaned four white plates and put them on the table. Cinnamon wondered why the man wore shades. It wasn't that sunny.

'I want extra onions and lemons. Don't forget, okay,' shouted one of the boys. He was plump and his head was shaven.

'You didn't pay the last few times. Are you going to pay for the previous times first or after breakfast?' asked Aditi. They ignored her and stared at their mobiles. 'Tell me, are you going to pay for the last few times now or later?' Aditi insisted.

'I don't know anything about that. We are coming here for the first time,' the man who wore shades replied arrogantly. Not giving up easily, Aditi repeated her question. 'What last few times money? What are you talking about, woman?' said one of the boys, suddenly slamming the stainless-steel glass on the table.

'Don't act too smart. You know well which money I'm talking about,' Aditi retorted.

'Calm your wife,' the man told to Santosh. Santosh put aside the huge tea ladle and came forward. 'Woman, learn to talk respectfully,' the big man warned.

'Don't act too smart with me. Are you going to pay now or later?' Aditi spoke fearlessly.

'You talk a lot. We can close down this bloody place if we want!' the big man threatened. The other people in the restaurant swivelled around to stare at the scene. The hair on Cinnamon's arms stood up.

Santosh intervened at this point. 'Please, come with me,' he said and took the man with black shades and gold chain and also one of the boys outside the restaurant. Aditi followed. Cinnamon stayed behind, though he desperately wanted to hear the conversation. There was some confabulation until the man finally grimaced and

मसाला भात
पापलेट
हलवा

took out from his shirt's front pocket a thick bundle of notes and handed out a couple.

'I hope the matter is settled now,' the big man exclaimed loudly. Santosh nodded his head with a slight smile. Afterwards, Aditi served the men extra lemons and onions. They ate the food and went off, but the man in the smart shoes tarried a while. He shook hands with both Aditi and Santosh.

'We are very sorry for what happened. They are still young, these boys. You know how it is at that age. It happens. Don't take it personally. You are our family,' he said.

'Yes, of course. Most arguments happen within a family,' Aditi observed.

He then looked curiously at Cinnamon. 'Who is this?' he asked, shaking hands with him.

Santosh quickly said, 'Our nephew.' Cinnamon thought it best to go along. Soon, the man sauntered off.

'Are you okay?' Cinnamon asked concernedly.

Aditi looked ahead and didn't answer. Her tone softened a little bit. 'When you run a restaurant, son, you have to treat every rascal with money like your own son-in-law. But nothing for you to worry about re,' she said and pinched his cheeks.

Cinnamon saw during the entire day how Aditi handled different types of customers expertly and efficiently. On several occasions, when nothing of what the customer wanted was available, she didn't let them go and convinced them to buy something else. Another time, Santosh informed a customer with a straight face that poha was not available when it actually was.

'Why did you do that kaka? Poha was available right?'

'Soon, Pintya will come. He always comes to have poha every day at this time,' replied Santosh.

Soon, Pintya came at around 4 p.m. He wore a carefully wrapped white turban and seemed to be one of their regular customers from the way he greeted them. Santosh told him about what had happened. Pintya said, chortling, 'You can still get these customers to pay you if you are forceful enough. But you know very well, there are some who won't pay at all, no matter what and how much you shout. You may have to pay them instead.' He winked and gave a belly-aching laugh and was joined by Aditi and the other customers. Even Santosh allowed himself a broad smile for the first time.

At night, when Cinnamon laid down on the satranji, next to Baba and Maa, he told them about the incident. They were shocked but not surprised.

'You find such characters everywhere and in every business. As business people, these are the challenges you have to face and overcome; there is no other option. There are times when I have gone through such experiences. But I must say, she is a fighter,' Baba remarked.

His back smarted for the first time from the hard floor and satranji. He looked around him—at the simple tiled roof, the walls, the wooden bed, and the rustic kitchen. He thought of the small village school, the rutted road leading to the village, and the simple homes of people. Suddenly, his home in Pune seemed so far away.

He thought of his birth mother, sitting in that small highway restaurant in one corner and dealing with countless rude customers. He replayed the entire scene in his mind. This time, he thought, they were able to make them cough up the money but there was no telling what would happen in the future. What if she had been the only person? What all must she have gone through in the process of establishing this modest restaurant? It made him see things in a new light from then on.

## *Chapter 15*

# Riding an Enfield

It Cinnamon's fourteenth birthday. That morning, he opened his eyes in anticipation of what the day had to offer. He took a bath, wore a kurta, and then Aditi and Maa did his aukshan. When Cinnamon entered the living room, there was a small cake on the table with fourteen candles and Baba, Maa, and Aditi stood around it. There was also lime juice, Coca Cola, samosas, kachourie, and some Khandeshi specialities.

'Happy birthday!' Baba, Maa, and Aditi congratulated Cinnamon and then they all hugged him tightly. The only gift was a set of sketch brushes and watercolours for painting. Seeing the art stationery, Cinnamon got an idea.

'Aai, I would like to draw you.' It was the first time he had called Aditi aai. Cinnamon took out his easel pad and all his art stationery. Aditi smiled but then changed her mind.

'I am not in a condition to be drawn. Wait. Let me get ready first,' she said and disappeared inside the room.

After fifteen or twenty minutes, Aditi came out and then sat on the floor in front of him. He couldn't tell what the difference was exactly, but she looked pleased. 'Now you can draw me. Draw properly. Okay, boy.'

With deft strokes, Cinnamon started outlining her. The difficulty was in drawing the clothes. It was challenging to capture the movement and the fluidity of the lugada—the sari worn by tribal women—wrapped between the knees. She also wore silver jewellery. Then, using the colour pencils, he filled in the colours at a basic level. He had seen the guys in front of the Jehangir Art Gallery in Mumbai fill up a blank page with a few strokes of their hands. A swish-swoosh here and then a swoosh-swish there and suddenly, the whole portrait was ready. One day, he dreamt, he would be as good as them, but for now, he had to practise.

After half an hour or so of relentless work, Cinnamon had a tolerable representation of his mother in front of him. He tore off the sheet and handed it over with a smile. Aditi stared at it for some time, before hugging him tightly. 'I will frame this and keep it on the wall here.'

Feeling somewhat proud of his skills, Cinnamon took out his sketch pad and wandered around the village, trying to capture the scenes from the village. White bullocks straining in the agriculture fields, schoolgirls wearing blue salwar kameezes and carrying their notebooks against their chests, women walking with stacks of firewood on their heads, all such scenes inspired Cinnamon's artistic side.

Cinnamon noticed a group of girls playing hopscotch. He gazed at them for a while. Then one of them stepped forward. She seemed to be the leader of the group. 'Hi, you want to play?'

Cinnamon felt embarrassed. No, I don't play these girlish games, he thought but didn't say anything.

'Why don't you open your mouth and say something?' she asked.

'His aai must have told him not to talk to us village children on his field trip here. Not good to talk to strangers. Poor boy,' the girl said, mimicking a grown woman's voice.

The other girls sniggered. Cinnamon felt the hair on his neck stand up. 'Do you make these stupid remarks only with newcomers to the village? Or are you always like this?' Cinnamon said, finally finding his voice.

When the other girls giggled, he knew his remark had hit home. 'Always like this!' they said in unison.

The leader of the group seemed momentarily at a loss for words. She made a face and stuck her tongue out in disgust. Cinnamon walked back, feeling happy that the conversation had come to an end. He went back home and sat for a while in a cross-legged position. He had become good at sitting this way, since coming to the village. He saw that Maa and Aditi were deep in conversation. Maa's Koregaon Park Marathi was undergoing a complete revolution. Then he heard the sound—thud-thud-thud! It could only be a Royal Enfield, he thought.

Aditi noticed the excitement on Cinnamon's face. 'Devendra, why don't you give Cinnamon a tour on your Enfield?' she said when Devendra walked in. 'Maybe, for thirty minutes?'

Cinnamon spoke up immediately, 'No, I want you to take me!'

Aditi grinned. 'You will enjoy a chakkar (round) with him,' she said confidently.

Devendra said briskly, 'Well I have time. It will give him a new experience.'

'Bring him back before it gets dark,' cautioned Baba.

'It's not Pune,' Aditi said dismissively. 'There are no safety problems here.'

'Bring him before it gets dark,' Baba repeated.

Devendra started the bike and they drove around the village. Cinnamon saw flocks of goats and sheep being taken down the village roads. The shepherds were behind them with long sticks calling out 'hut-hut-hut.' The sky had turned to a brilliant orange.

'This is the local government school,' Devendra said. It was a nondescript, yellow coloured two-storey building. Why do government schools and buildings everywhere look the same, Cinnamon thought. There must be some law to that effect.

'You came here after graduation?' Cinnamon asked.

'Not really. After graduation, I was working in a big IT company in Hyderabad for four years and came to realise that the nine-to-five job was not suiting me. So, I left that job.'

'After that?'

'I came here to help the local people. And here I am now.'

Devendra greeted a man who was wearing brown khaki trousers and had bushy sideburns. 'He's one of the teachers here,' Devendra explained. Cinnamon wondered what exactly he taught.

Cinnamon's mind went back to his own school. The big airy classrooms with only about 20-25 students in every class. How much personal attention was given to every student. How the teachers would follow up at PTA meetings about his performance in every subject. The school's attempts to push the students into Olympiads, elocution contests, sports, and other activities so that they could put up news about 'Achievements of students' on the notice board.

Cinnamon tried to imagine studying in this small classroom but couldn't do so. 'Is it a Marathi medium school?' asked Cinnamon.

'No. It's a Chinese medium school,' Devendra replied with a straight face.

Devendra would stop leisurely, pluck ripe bora from trees, and bite into them with relish. Cinnamon saw groups of men, wearing white topis and phetas on their heads, sitting under a big tree, and chatting in the local tribal dialects. A few sipped a clear drink and smoked beedis. The younger farmers read Marathi newspapers while the older farmers chatted and played cards. A couple of women were paying respects at the local village temple. It was a different kind of lifestyle.

Crickets had started their khir-khir. The birds had fallen silent; a sign that darkness was on its way. When they left the school, Cinnamon finally let out the question that had been brewing inside him for long. 'Devendra, people from this place or other such places migrate to big cities like Pune or Surat. They live in small shanties near the railway tracks to fulfil their dream of living in a big city. Then why did you leave a high paying job in Hyderabad to come to this place?' Cinnamon was mortified at how rude that question sounded. I am behaving like those nosy TV reporters, he thought. Next thing, I'll be sticking a mike in his face and asking, 'How does it feel to be working in a village?'

Without replying, Devendra went towards a small kirana store. The counters were stacked with plastic containers with red lids, chewing gum, biscuits, khari, rolls, and jam naankatai. The shopkeeper greeted him warmly and gave him a tiny cup of tea in a white paper cup. Devendra was a newcomer and these signs of acknowledgement were important to him. Cinnamon noticed that Devendra didn't pay for anything.

'Do you have an account with the shop?' Cinnamon asked and Devendra shook his head casually.

'It's a good question,' he said whipping out the beedi and lighting it. Blowing stylish smoke rings so close to a school wasn't the most praiseworthy conduct but

Cinnamon didn't say anything. There were no students to be corrupted.

'I suppose you don't smoke beedis?' Devendra said with a totally straight face. Cinnamon shook his head, not seeing the relevance of the question.

'No, I don't smoke at all,' Cinnamon said irritatedly. 'Bhaiya, it's not good for your health. Why do you smoke beedis?'

'I smoke beedis to support my fellow Indians. I hope you understand.'

Cinnamon stared at him suspiciously.

'Beedis are a totally Indian industry and not promoted by any MNC or foreign company. We, the Indian youth, must support Indian products and services and create jobs for Indians and not run madly after foreign goods or companies. Beedis are totally natural. Moreover, the paper is rolled by women and gives employment to the very poor. Unlike cigarettes, they don't have ammonia which make them addictive. Didn't your history teacher teach you about the Swadeshi movement or about encouraging local industries? Well, this is my contribution to local industries in India in my own tiny way. I am not smoking beedis for myself actually; it's only for my countrymen and women.'

Despite his best efforts, Cinnamon couldn't restrain giggling. 'You should be a politician or a TV anchor, bhaiya,' he said finally. 'You can convince anybody of anything.'

Devendra turned away as if to brush off the compliment but Cinnamon caught the pride in his eyes.

More than once during the trip, he noticed that behind that impassive exterior, Devendra was a man of great vanity.

'Bhaiya, you haven't answered the question,' said Cinnamon.

Devendra pressed his old Nike sneakers firmly into the soil. He watched the smoke curl up from his cigarette before speaking. 'Honestly, this kind of work suits me more. I don't need to pay half my salary for a house I only came back to sleep in at night and for a car I only drove to work. I don't think I have sacrificed anything. I have experienced everything in life, both the good and bad, when I did social work in my college and as an IT engineer before that. The things I have done would be enough for a book or a movie. In fact, this place and life suit me more.'

'If everyone goes to a big city, what will you do here, bhaiya? What will you do the whole day sitting here? Smoke beedis and play cards?' Cinnamon yelled.

Devendra grinned wickedly, showing off his yellowing teeth. Cinnamon winced. Whatever exciting things Devendra had learnt as a student of social work and as an IT engineer, brushing his teeth regularly was clearly not one of them.

'Man, you ask so many questions one after the other. Let's say there are 140 crore people in India. Now, imagine one day in the distant future, 95 per cent of them do not need help of any kind. This still leaves crores of people, which is more than the population of most countries.

'Come on man, look at this beautiful and unexplored district of Nandurbar—the trees, the pure air and water, the forested hills, the clean streams and ponds, and the healthy village food, grown without using any chemicals. You can dip your hands into a cool, bubbling stream in the hills here and drink it. There is no need for Aquaguard and Eureka Forbes. Look at the warm and simple people of Nandurbar here. How genuinely hospitable they are. There is no fake self-centred hospitality that you get in big cities. Moreover, think about what you and I have missed out, living and working all our lives in our concrete bird nests. Isn't that why people like you and me pay lots of money to go on treks and camping trips, to sleep inside uncomfortable sleeping bags in places with no electricity and bad roads? So that we can experience this life for a short time? If I can experience it for free, what have I really given up?' he said and thumped Cinnamon on the back to assert the point of his argument.

The logic could not be refuted easily, though Cinnamon felt there were countless loopholes in what Devendra had said. He couldn't put it into words what they were. It was like every time; words had failed him again.

Sensing he had won the argument, Devendra stubbed out his beedi. 'Come sir, let's go. It will get dark very soon. By the time you finish asking all your questions, it will be midnight and then your Baba would hang me by my collar. You should be one of those infuriating TV reporters when you grow up. That's your ideal profession,' he quipped.

Cinnamon laughed. Devendra had certainly read his mind. 'Yeah, I guess I should definitely become a journalist right. Imagine getting paid to ask questions. I could do it all day, all night. It would be my dream job.'

Devendra then said in a very serious tone, 'Waise, I must tell you, smoking is an absolutely terrible habit. It's completely unhealthy. Never do it in future also.'

'Don't worry bhaiya. I am absolutely not interested. But if ever, I think about smoking, I will remember you and your wise words.' Devendra's face had a strong 'Oh really?' look on it. 'Bhaiya, I will recall how skinny and weak you look; that memory itself will be enough to stop me. Maybe, they should put your photo instead on those cigarette packs. It can definitely discourage people,' he said and guffawed. 'You'll become famous as well.'

'Chalo, chalo,' Devendra replied, chuckling. He then switched on the bike and kicked the starter. Cinnamon didn't get on the bike and kept staring at him fixedly.

'What happened, sir? Any more questions?'

'This is your Enfield?'

'It is now, Maharaj. I can't provide you a car. Sorry.'

'I want to ride the bike this time.'

Devendra raised his eyebrows. 'Ride where? You aren't strong enough to ride an Enfield. Why not start with a Scooty first?'

Cinnamon punched Devendra in the shoulder with force. 'Is that strong enough?'

'Well, you have some strength after all,' remarked Devendra, wincing.

'I want to ride,' Cinnamon persisted.

Devendra slid off the bike with a sigh and held out the keys. Cinnamon took the keys excitedly and hopped onto the bike.

'I want to ride the bike,' Devendra mimicked Cinnamon. 'Start the bike first.' Cinnamon kicked and kicked many times but the bike refused to respond. To add insult to injury, the bike's front wheel scornfully swung away from him. 'Can't manage it?' Devendra said with a tone of smugness.

Annoyed, Cinnamon put all his energy in that last kick and to his delight, came the familiar sound—the unmistakable and cheerful thud-thud-thud. 'Let's go!' he shouted. Devendra got on bike and off they went around the village. Devendra's deft and strong hands guided the bike expertly. Boys and girls waved to him, called him out, and hooted loudly.

They drove around the village and finally, rode towards Aditi Gavit's hut. Cinnamon shouted so loudly that faint sounds reached his parents in the thatched hut and immediately, they came out and cheered. The incongruous sight of a tall boy and a lanky man sitting behind him looked delightful—a boy who was half man and a man who was half boy.

There was a final surprise at night, after dinner. Aditi sang a number of tribal songs and patiently explained their meanings. After that, the elders talked about the different situations and aspects of the rural life: how a woman felt about getting married, the challenges of migration in the area, the simple, millet-based diet of the area, the eager anticipation of the monsoon rains, and songs of devotion to the tribal deities. Listening to them, Cinnamon felt that basic human emotions, regardless of language, culture, and background, were exactly the same. Later that night, as he snuggled himself in his satranji, he felt it was the best birthday he had ever had.

*Chapter 16*

# Candle Light

After Cinnamon went to sleep, Aditi spoke with Baba and Maa. They sat on the floor as the pleasant breeze from the open windows made the candles flicker. Aditi talked a lot about her life, why she gave up Cinnamon for adoption, and the problems she had had to overcome. As they were talking, Aditi paused for a while and stared out of the window into the darkness. Then she asked, 'I have a question for you.'

Cinnamon's Baba nodded in silence.

'Why did you let him see me?'

'I guess because I am his Baba. I want my child to be happy,' Baba said with a smile. Aditi looked at him keenly. 'From the time he came to know that he was adopted, he wanted to know who his parents were. So, I thought that bringing him here would be the best gift for him.'

'Then why do I keep thinking that there is more to this story than you are revealing? What if Cinnamon does not go back with you? How could you take that risk? It cannot be that affluent people like you came to this isolated village only because a boy wanted to see his birth mother!'

'He's our son, not any other boy. We have already told you the reason! Or, are you saying that we are lying to you?' asked Maa petulantly.

'Don't say whatever you want. I never said you are lying,' Aditi responded, her eyes were flashing with rage.

Baba intervened in the argument. 'It's fine. I am sure she doesn't mean it that way,' he said.

'I didn't mean it that way. But I really feel that there is more to the story,' Aditi said. 'I have seen certain things which have made me very uncomfortable.'

'Seen?' Baba said, looking at her. 'What did you see? What do you mean?'

'Well . . . tonight . . . before he went to sleep . . .' Aditi looked at her husband once and continued after she got an approving nod from him, 'I saw him stumbling around when he went to fetch himself a glass of water at night. And not only that, he did not even respond in one go when I called out to him asking whether he needed any help. I have observed this several times.'

'You are . . .' Maa began to speak but immediately, Baba held her hand and stopped her.

He then took a deep breath and then started speaking. 'We have noticed his inability to see properly at night for some time. His hearing is weak too. In fact, often we found ourselves repeating instructions to him multiple times. Even his teachers would sometimes tell us that there were times, in the classroom, when he didn't seem to hear what was being said. Initially we disregarded it, as teenagers are stubborn, but the condition became worse with time. The doctors prescribed him some medicines and for a time, it had a positive effect. But since the last year, it has become more prominent. This time, I consulted one of the best doctors in Delhi. I took all his records with me as well.' He saw that Aditi was looking at him fearfully; her brows had creased. He swallowed hard before speaking, 'It turns out that Cinnamon has a rare disease, unfortunately. He has been diagnosed with type 3 of the Usher syndrome.'

'Usher? What is that?' Aditi asked worriedly.

'It is a genetic disorder. In most cases, neither of the parents have it. It affects both hearing and sight. I read everything that I could about this rare syndrome. It is a rare medical condition that roughly affects only three to ten kids in one lakh children. By the time the child becomes a teenager, he generally loses both hearing and vision, though the severity of it varies from one child to the other,' Baba said with tears rolling down his cheeks. He then handed over some medical articles in Marathi to Aditi. 'There is a little bit of good news for us,' he continued. 'Cinnamon's condition is not so severe. The doctor feels that although his sight is very likely to stay for many years, and in fact, well into his forties, his hearing will diminish much more rapidly, and he would probably lose his hearing in some years.'

'Is that why you . . .'

'I had to give him a chance to hear the voices of his

birth father and mother. For any person, these are the two most beautiful voices in the world. I could not take that right away from him. And time was running out for us. When I came to know that his birth father had already died, I realised I couldn't delay. I wanted him to hear at least his mother's voice. You will recall, I had asked whether you had any records of his father's voice.'

'And is there any cure?' Aditi asked, her voice shaking.

He shook his head. 'As of now, nothing. Work is going on of course. A child can get hearing implants, so that will help of course. But, overall, the child and the family will need to make lifestyle changes to carry on with life. The fact that he will retain his eyesight for a long time is truly a saving grace.'

Aditi was crying by now. Basundhara was by her side. 'When I heard the news, I was as shocked as you are now,' she said and hugged Aditi tightly.

'But . . . does he know about this?' Santosh asked who had hitherto remained silent. Tears were rolling down his cheeks as well. Cinnamon's Baba shook his head.

'When will you tell him?'

Baba stared out of the window into the never-ending darkness. 'We will tell him when the time is right,' he said finally.

## *Chapter 17*

# Going Home

*'In every conceivable manner, the family is link to our past, bridge to our future.'*

—Alex Haley

The next morning, all hands were on deck. Cinnamon didn't show much interest in packing and Baba and Maa had to do everything together.

As Cinnamon was lying on bed, Aditi came and put her calloused hands on his head and said, 'Stay in touch, my boy. Look at you. You have all the opportunities in the world to study and do well. Get a good job and then become a big officer. I will come to see you then. Your mother will still be here, running this small hotel. Do your best. I am with you always. Keep visiting me.' Her eyes shone with love and affection.

Baba and Devendra had made arrangements to go to the Nandurbar station together. From there, they would take the train to Pune.

When they reached the Nandurbar station, everyone heaved a sigh of relief after realising that their train had, mercifully, arrived well in advance. They then made their way to their respective compartment and after placing the luggage, they decided to spend the remaining time inside the train. Aditi and Cinnamon sat on one side of the berth, while Maa and Baba sat on the other side. For the first time, Cinnamon realised how tired both of them looked. Years had been added to their faces in the last few days.

'From the time he was a small child, Cinnamon wanted to meet both his father and mother. I never thought it would be possible till he turned eighteen, as the rules don't permit it. We feel a tremendous sense of gratitude to meet you. We can see that his mother is a brave and tenacious woman and I am sure his father was no less,' Baba said with emotion and feeling. 'I can't even imagine how many challenges you have faced in your life, from losing your husband at an early age to having to relinquish your son and carving out your own business in these difficult circumstances. I wish that Cinnamon has some of your qualities when he becomes an adult.' For Cinnamon, it was rare to see Baba speaking with so much emotion.

Aditi clasped her hands and said, 'You also did a very great thing too by adopting him and giving him a chance to have a good life. I will always be very thankful for that.'

Maa shook her head vehemently. 'We haven't done anything great or noble. One can have a child through biological ways or one can adopt a child. We chose to adopt and we did what any normal parents would do for their children. That's all there is to it. There is no need to praise us in any way.' Aditi wiped her eyes.

'Aai, I will keep visiting, don't worry,' exclaimed Cinnamon loudly. 'You too come and visit us at our home.'

'Your home,' she said quietly.

'Now it's your home too,' he declared. She looked back at him but said nothing.

'If you had more time, you could have visited Toranmal, the temple in Prakasha, and the hot springs in Unapdev,' Aditi said.

'Some other time. We have our own talkative hot spring here. Meet us when you come to Pune. You have our address and phone numbers also,' said Maa.

Cinnamon knew that the train would soon start its journey to Pune and Aditi would have to get off. But he didn't want her to go. 'Can't you come along?' he asked, hoping she would say yes.

'I will come. But not immediately. Not immediately, but soon. Be well, son!'

Soon, the train siren rang and Aditi got up to leave. Cinnamon accompanied her to the railway platform. He then hugged her deeply and held her for some time.

'Your train will leave and you will be stranded here. I don't mind that of course,' she said with tears in her eyes. Cinnamon was crying as well.

'I will keep visiting,' he said. 'I won't stop coming now. I promise this. Promise.' He hugged her again and then climbed onto the train door step, just as it started moving. He stood at the train door and waved at her until he could not see her anymore. He was unable to break this trance and kept standing at the train door, crying his heart out.

After some time, he made his way back to his berth and sat between Baba and Maa.

A few minutes into the journey, the rain started pouring down. The majestic tree-covered mountain ranges of North Maharashtra rolled by. Cinnamon was heartbroken by the fact that he would never meet his birth father. But he had got many photos of his father that he had kept with himself.

Baba and Maa called Aditi a brave woman. Perhaps, that's also what bravery meant, he reflected. Not just the heroic acts that were reported in the news, that got you bravery awards from the president, or that went viral on WhatsApp and Facebook. Bravery was also in the small, everyday things you did in your life to keep going from day to day. He realised that surviving in difficult circumstances was in itself an act of bravery.

Cinnamon was glad that he was able to meet and know more about his birth mother and father. The conceptions he had of them were gone and in their place, there was a much better reality. He realised that his birth parents were genuine and warm people rooted in traditional values, and that with much effort, they had carved out a life for themselves. They faced tremendous difficulties in life but still managed to keep a smile on their faces. In their own way, they were very much people to be proud of.

As the city started to come into view, a lone ray of sunlight struck out defiantly between the grey clouds, as if ushering in the promise of a new future. Cinnamon knew his life would always have a lot of questions but also realised that his parents would always help in answering them. He had two sets of parents now, and he would always hold both close to him. They were a part of his life. He had accepted this.

After a long journey, the train finally halted with a long, angry hiss. Cinnamon grabbed the luggage and put the straps of the bag on his sturdy shoulders. He turned to Baba and Maa.

'Come Baba. Come Maa. Let's go home.'

# A Note on the Book - I

Why does anyone have a passion for writing? Why does anyone write? It is largely due to the desire to understand the existence of the self and its relation to the larger world around them. In my view, writing is not about competing, earning rewards, or satisfying anyone. It is essentially about expressing oneself in a holistic and creative way to understand, analyse, accept, and reject the realities of life.

Through their words, writers influence readers and even change their thoughts and behaviour at an individual level as well as on a larger scale. Creative writers have done this for thousands of years, in different parts of the world. In that sense, the power of creative writing is over and above any religion, nation, political authority, and belief system. It is above any specific 'ism'. This explains why political systems all over the world have routinely suppressed writers and denied them creative freedom, as they are only too aware of the threat these independent writers pose. Throughout recorded human history, writers have faced these severe challenges. This is all too visible in many parts of today's world as well.

Yet, in every generation, there are a few people who push themselves to become writers while being fully aware of the difficulties that lie ahead. It can be said that these people are born writers—writers by nature and not purely by choice. In my humble opinion, Vikas Prakash Joshi is one such among them.

In an era where writing is increasingly seen as a professional career option or a way of attracting attention to oneself, it is important to remember that a writer must first and foremost be passionate about writing itself. It is this passion that we can see in Vikas's book in which he chose a complex and technical subject like Usher syndrome, otherwise unknown to most, and weave a story around it. He has taken pains to find the personal stories of those suffering from this disease, as well as consult the relevant authorities and experts. Usher syndrome is a rare, genetic disorder that causes progressive hearing and sight loss for which, at present, there is no cure. In this regard, Helen Keller has shown that the burdens of sensory limitations can be overcome. She was deaf and blind but she still managed to overcome all the odds and become a world-renowned writer and activist. It is said that she had no idea of written language and only had the haziest idea of spoken language. She nevertheless vividly described the feeling of water when it ran over her hands, showing us all the power of the human imagination.

I shall not review the book or express my views on its merits or demerits; this is a task always best left to the reader. Rather, as a senior poet, prolific writer, and socio-cultural activist with decades of experience, I will state that it is not merely enough to have a passion for writing. A writer must also learn and apply the tools and craft of his trade. These tools include the ability to create an entire world believable to us and based on real life, yet much more attractive and appealing. The language used, values, style, setting, characterisation, images, flow, and world-building are very important in this regard. It is, in essence, about the ability to create worlds which we want to live in, about the ability to create characters who we care about deeply, and about transforming the personal thoughts of the writer or real-life experiences into such expressions that appeal to a larger audience. This is the benchmark by which any writer in any language has and always will be judged.

In his very first book, Vikas has shown himself capable of doing all this, competently and effectively. He has created confidence that he is indeed well on his way to becoming a renowned writer. I am confident this will happen in the future. My blessings are with him in his journey as a writer and for life, for this book, and for all his future writings as well.

—Dr Shripad Bhalchandra Joshi

Eminent writer, poet, socio-cultural activist, and former president, Akhil Bharatiya Marathi Sahitya Mahamandal and Akhil Bharatiya Marathi Sahitya Sammelan (All India Marathi Literary Federation and Literary Conference)

# A Note on the Book – II

'He just saw it as a natural part of his identity.' 'If I am adopted, there is nothing I can do about it.' When I read these two sentences at different moments in the story, I fully identified with Cinnamon. He is referring to his adoption but I related as an Usher syndrome companion. It is about acceptance, which is a stage of grief we all face at some point in life.

Cinnamon learns through the love of his parents that adoption is not something wrong or bad in any way. It is just as it is. It should be the same with Usher syndrome and many other disabilities. There are different types of Usher syndrome and in some cases, the hearing and vision loss are severe and they truly influence daily and social life. Dealing with the degeneration of sight, hearing, or both needs a constant adjustment of habits, movements, tools, and devices. No more riding the bike, no more driving the car, no more reading a book. It is hard, no doubt, but on the other hand, it improves one's resilience and propels them to achieve their dreams. Cinnamon and Vikas are like this. The first wishes to meet his birth parents at any cost and the second always wanted to write a book, until he did. Usher syndrome is also this. A burning fire that gives you no choice but to pursue your goals, as you may not see or hear the same way for much longer.

I had to read this book with no breaks as I wanted to know how the young boy would receive the diagnosis. Most of those with Usher can relate to Cinnamon as we slowly find out that something is not right. Maa and Baba will find the best way to inform him. They will support him as they have always done. They will do it when they feel that they are ready. This is what I suggest to the dozens of mothers reaching out to NoisyVision with the fear that they will not be able to go through all the challenges, with the fear that their child will not be able to cope with this syndrome. Today, thanks to this book, we have the chance to say to all other Usher patients and families that we will make it, we will face it, and hopefully, one day we will cure it.

On the other hand, this book is a unique opportunity to inform others about the existence of this disease and the importance of understanding its consequences to avoid prejudices. My heartfelt gratitude goes to Vikas. He had no connection to Usher syndrome till he read these words in a newspaper article. He took it upon himself the challenge to write a story and to inform readers in a country where there is very little information available on this subject.

The way he writes immerses the reader in the story and it is impossible not to identify with the characters.

Through his narration, Vikas also takes the reader deep inside Indian culture and Indian cuisine. I could smell every single dish; I could nearly taste the food. I wanted to drop the book and run outside looking for an Indian restaurant. Even more, it made me want to fly to India, hug Cinnamon, Maa, and Baba, and sit at the table with them, and get to know them as people. This is what a good book does. It takes you into a different world, a new world, where the senses are so stimulated that it does not matter how much you can hear or see, as it is all within your heart and mind.

—Dario Sorgato, Italy
Founder and chairman, NoisyVision

# Acknowledgements

Whenever I finished reading a book as a child, I would always think, 'The book is good but why are there so many names in the Acknowledgements section?' Now that I have written my first book, I know exactly why.

First and foremost, I would like to thank you, dear reader, for picking up this book. Writing a book is a lonely, never-ending ride and thus every reader who picks up your book makes all the work worthwhile.

To my parents, Aai and Baba, and my elder brother Madhav. Without them, this book wouldn't have been possible. Aai suffered through countless drafts but never lost hope, despite all the problems she herself was going through. She has always been my first reader and critic, an extremely unenviable task. I am really grateful to them for always being there for me and giving wings to my dreams.

Thanks to Ashok Chopra, Aditya Jarial, and the entire Hay House team for their faith in this unusual book and for publishing it. It is an honour to have an internationally acclaimed publisher like Hay House for my first book.

My gratitude for guiding and dealing patiently with a first-time author.

To Nishad Takley, my uncle, who always strongly nurtured and supported my interest in writing. I have spent numerous hours in his home, reading from his eclectic and diverse home library.

To Dr Shripad Bhalchandra Joshi for his lucid and inspiring foreword.

I am deeply indebted to Niloufer Wadia, an award-winning and prolific illustrator, for all the illustrations and cover artwork that have added immeasurable value to the book. I am sure you enjoyed her work.

This book is dedicated to all those with Usher syndrome as well as to those who are adopted or will be adopted. I request you to consider this your book.

To Chris and Molly Sano from Seattle and Steve and Christine Myers from Visual Bucket List Foundation, USA, whose stories planted the initial seed for this book. This is their book in a very real sense. I am immensely obliged to the large number of adoptive parents, children, and organisations who very generously gave me their time and input. In particular, I wish to thank people at Atmaja in Kolkata including Nilanjana Gupta, Buchi Gupta, Swarup Naskar, Anhiti Naskar, Sheemantika Nag, Anup Dewanji, and Sanjay Sikdar. To T. V. S. Shekhar from the Bangalore-based Sudatta Adoptive Parents Association, Ketki Ovhal, and Priya Ramanathan. To Savita Nagpurkar from the Indian Association for Promotion of Adoption and Child Welfare (IAPA). To

Dr Prajakta Kulkarni and Balasaheb Dattatray Warule from Snehalaya in Ahmednagar.

To Prasanna Kumar Shirol and Dipanjana Dutta De from Organisation for Rare Diseases in India. To Nancy O'Donnell and Nilam Agarwal from Usher Syndrome Coalition, Dario Sorgato from NoisyVision, Divya, Abhay, Aruna Goel, Elias Kabakov from The Centre for Deaf-Blind Persons of the Beth David Institute, Israel, and Dr Raj Apte from Washington University, St. Louis, USA. I extend my deepest thanks to all of you for all your extremely helpful inputs and assistance. Your stories of courage and capability will always be etched in my mind.

To Roxana Kalyanwala from the Pune-based Bharatiya Samaj Seva Kendra, for patiently explaining to me various social, legal, and cultural aspects of adoption.

To Preeta and Aeisha Bhuyan for their insights into the lifestyle and psychology of teenagers and pre-teens.

To Dr Sanyogita Nadkarni and Dr Gauri Choudhari for their invaluable inputs on counselling and child psychology.

To Neelima Jorwar, Milind Patil, Girdhan Pawara, and Ashwini Kumar for providing me with insightful information about Nandurbar and the Adivasi communities in particular. My visits to Nandurbar were made possible by Ashwini's hospitality.

To Moitrayee Bhaduri, Dr Sourya Das, Joyeeta, and Basudhara Choudhuri for their insights into Bengali culture and lifestyle and for going through the relevant sections with a keen eye.

My profound thanks to all the amazing, eminent writers from India and abroad, from as many as thirty countries, who graciously supported this book, even before it found a publisher. This kind of international appreciation and genuine feedback for improvement not only sharpened the manuscript but was indeed a dream come true for a debutant writer.

It is through constructive feedback, editing, and rewriting that a messy first draft truly blossoms and transforms into a story. The first feedback that one gets is therefore very important. My love and gratitude to Ujjwala Samarth who gave many valuable early inputs. To Mini Shrinivasan, Aditi Raman Sridhar, and Neil Doshi for their encouraging feedback that motivated me to keep going and gave me the confidence that my story had value. To Arun Bhave and Aditi Ray Bose for investing countless hours in evaluating and refining the manuscript.

Many thanks to Dr Sucharita Dutta Asane, Anand Borse, Dr Vilas Salunke, Dr Pervin Saket, Neetu Ralhan, Sujata Raye, Kritika Rajat Sharma, Irina Papancheva, Pradnya Malandkar, Abha Iyengar, Harshal Khade, and Dario Sorgato whose editorial advice and criticism enriched the book tremendously.

To Etisha Botre and Anagha Karhade for carefully proofreading the manuscript.

To Ketki Akut Ovhal who wrote the beautiful poem in chapter 4 and for generally being a very supportive and fun person.

To Dr Shraddha Satav for insights on sports at the school level, as a mother of a competitive sportsman.

A special thanks to Dr Kelly Mekdeci, the late Dr Patrick Fredericks, Mrs Pramila Mathews, my wonderful school English teachers. Besides them, I would also like thank my English teachers at the Symbiosis College of Arts and Commerce and the faculty at Asian College of Journalism, Chennai. I am truly blessed to have many outstanding English teachers throughout my school and college days, who nurtured my love for reading and writing. They may consider this book as a guru dakshina.

To Sashi Kumar, the director of the ACJ, for choosing me as the recipient of the prestigious South Asia Foundation Madanjeet Singh Scholarship.

To Mrs Sujata Raye, who was a dream mentor and gave me the rare and golden opportunity to write a weekly column at just eighteen years of age.

My deep appreciation to Rahul Badami of Pune Writers Group for his assistance on countless occasions.

To all my friends and associates, who despite hearing 'I have still not finished the book' countless times through the last few years never discouraged me at any time.

To all delivery associates who will go out in all conditions, rain or shine, to ensure that my book reaches its readers.

Long as this list is, there are so many others that it is simply impossible to mention all of them here. Sir Isaac Newton once said that if he could see further than others, it was only due to standing on the shoulders of giants. By extension, I do believe that this quote is applicable to every area of human life and to all achievements. I stand on your shoulders and my deep gratitude to you all.

# A Word from the Author

What do you want to be when you grow up?' My answer to this age-old question, as a child, jumped around a lot—from being Spiderman, a chocolate factory employee, public speaker, and magician—but there has always been one constant: I wanted to write a book and be a writer. I remember craning my neck to look at books on my school library's shelves and dreaming that one day, my name too would be on the spine of some book. But as I grew older and got caught up in life's endless tasks, this dream fell by the wayside for a long time. Finally, in 2017, I decided to stop waiting for destiny and get down to making my own fate.

I have put my entire journey down here, for aspiring writers to have a crystal-clear idea of how challenging this journey is. The world contains countless topics and yet every aspiring writer inevitably faces the dreaded question: 'What do I write about?' I started and stopped writing at least a few hundred times as none of my ideas seemed to have book potential. Finally, I zeroed in on one idea, which I felt was at least going somewhere. I started and stopped writing at least another hundred times as I had great difficulty taking things forward beyond a few pages. After God alone knows how many more attempts, the story started moving. After countless stops and starts and occasions where the book was repeatedly shelved, the manuscript was completed. I sent it to many different publishers and got rejected so many times that I lost count. For a time, I abandoned the file in the dark corners of my laptop. I never quite gave up hope though, as I had to get this book out in the world. I reworked the manuscript, round after round. Over time, a number of publishers, small and big, across the country slowly agreed to take it up. Post that, there was considerably more reworking and rewriting phases; practically speaking, much of the manuscript was rewritten and revisions went on forever. It finally got to the point where eight different traditional publishers made offers on a book by a first-time author, despite the huge post pandemic slump in publishing.

From the beginning, I was clear that I did not want to create a campus story, an autobiographical work, or a mythology derived tale (though I probably will do all of these in future). I wished to create awareness and inform the reader about ideas, disabilities, and geographies he or she may not be aware of. Fiction is a very good vehicle for talking about difficult concepts in an attractive and engaging manner. The book was challenging to write as it weaved together not only two different concepts, adoption and Usher syndrome, but also very distinct geographical and cultural regions, namely Pune, Kolkata, and Nandurbar along with a few references to other places. As far as another central idea of the book is concerned, adoption in India is a concept that is very familiar to us through our mythology. We are well aware of the stories of Krishna, Sita, Karna, and Shakuntala from our childhood days. In modern times, books by Deepa Balsavar, Nandana Dev Sen, and Lakshmi Giri, to name a few, have explored the theme of adoption with humour and sensitivity. The award-winning and acclaimed Oscar-nominated movie, *Lion,* also comes to mind. It is my hope that this book too would be a valuable addition to the emerging corpus in the literature on adoption in India and abroad, at a time when Indian society's attitude to adoption is changing for the better.

With respect to the Usher syndrome, I first came across the mention of this syndrome in a small article in the daily newspaper. It started a train of thought in my mind. After reading about it on offline and online portals, and interacting with those with this syndrome and those working in this area, I realised that there was no awareness about this disease among the general public in India. I immediately decided that I would play a role in changing this situation for the better. I am proud that this may well be the first book of its kind that highlights Usher syndrome in India. It is my fond hope that you will take a look at the organisations doing good work in both these areas—adoption and Usher syndrome—after reading this book and see how you can help them in any way possible.

To quote the legendary author, Dr Rudine Sims Bishop, I hope that the book has provided both a mirror to reflect the reader's experiences and a window to provide a glimpse of another world. How much I have succeeded in that task is, of course, left entirely to the reader to judge.

In conclusion, whenever I write anything, I am always reminded of a child standing or sitting at the train door, on a long journey, watching his lively surroundings whizzing by him with wide-open eyes. His parents sleep soundly inside the coach. He is curious and keenly observant about the world going by in front of him. However, this curiosity is not equal to gullibility. The child is not naïve; he or she is fully aware of the dangers that the world and people around can pose to him. It is this wide-eyed sense of curiosity and wonder, strongly underpinned by realism and shrewdness, that I have tried to capture in this story. This sense has shaped the faintest glimmer of an idea in my mind into a fully finished product in your hands.

It has been a maddening, unpredictable, endless, frustrating, enjoyable, tiring, greatly enriching, but ultimately, a very humbling and deeply fulfilling adventure.

*Vikas Prakash Joshi*

Vikas Prakash Joshi

A-Z

# Glossary

1. Aaho: Way of calling to someone in Marathi
2. Abhinandan: Congratulations in Marathi
3. Aai: Mother in Marathi
4. Ajoba and Aaji: Grandmother and grandfather in Marathi
5. Amer tock: Bengali dal that includes raw mangoes
6. Amras: Sweet mango pulp (a popular sweet dish in Maharashtra)
7. Aukshan: The ritual of waving a lit lamp in front of a deity or person
8. Baba: Father in Marathi and Bengali
9. Bakarwadi: A spicy tea-time snack made from gram flour
10. Bal mithai: A dark fudge-like sweet made from khoa and white sugar
11. Banyan: Vest
12. Batatachi bhaji: Fried potatoes (Maharashtrian cuisine)
13. Beta: Son

14. Bhaiyya: Brother in Hindi
15. Bhajan: Devotional song
16. Bhindi: Ladies' finger
17. Chai: Tea
18. Chaklis: A spicy snack, generally spiral in shape, made from rice flour and a mix of lentils and spice
19. *Champak*: A popular children's magazine in India
20. Chirer pulao: A popular Bengali dish made with flat, beaten rice
21. Daroon: Very good
22. Deed shaana: An insult in Marathi that roughly means being half-witted
23. Didi maa and dada moshay: Grandmother and grandfather in Bengali
24. Didi: Sister
25. Doodhwala: Milkman
26. Gadhav: Donkey in Marathi
27. Ghas phus: Term used for vegetarian food and often used in a sarcastic way
28. Kadubole: Someone who speaks bitterly
29. Istriwala: The person who irons clothes
30. Jhal muri: A popular street food made with puffed rice, spices, and vegetables
31. Kadu: Sour
32. Kaka and kaku: Paternal uncle and aunt (also used when speaking to older people)

33. Kakad aarti: Very early morning Hindu religious ceremony at the Shirdi Temple
34. Kakdi: Cucumber
35. Karela: Bitter gourd
36. Khichadi: A one pot dish generally made from rice and lentils
37. Kirana store: General store
38. Kol baalish: Cylindrical pillow, popular in West Bengal
39. Kosha Mangsho: Mutton curry, prepared with potatoes (Bengali cuisine)
40. Lakdi Ki Kathi: An iconic children's song from the Hindi movie, *Masoom*
41. Lambu: Tall
42. Maharaj: Ruler or king
43. Maidan: Field or ground, often used for outdoor games
44. Mame bhau: Maternal uncle's son
45. Mangal karyalaya: Marriage hall in Marathi
46. Motu: Fat
47. Mulgi: Girl in Marathi
48. Namaskar: A form of greeting in India
49. Nimbu-pani: Lemonade
50. Oye: Hey in Hindi
51. Paaji: A colloquial term used for people from Punjab

52. Pahaat: Early morning classical music session, common in winter in Pune
53. Pallu: The end portion of a sari
54. Papad: Poppadom
55. Pedhas: Popular sweet in India made of khoa, sugar, and saffron
56. Peru: Guava
57. Poha: A popular breakfast dish made with flat, beaten rice
58. Ponk: A popular fried snack made from sorghum
59. Pork vindaloo: A spicy pork dish, popular in the Indian state of Goa
60. Purano Sei Diner Kotha: A popular Bengali song based on the lyrics of Rabindranath Tagore
61. Pyaji: A deep fried pakora made from onion and flour
62. Raja: A term of endearment used for children
63. Rosogolla: A round white sweet made of cottage cheese dipped in sugar syrup
64. Saheb: Sir
65. Satranji: Floor mat
66. Shakha pola: Bangles worn by married Bengali women
67. Swadeshi movement: A movement which was aimed at promoting Indian made goods, during the period of British colonial rule in India

68. Thulabhaaram: Weighing scale
69. Upma: A popular breakfast dish, especially in Maharashtra, Gujarat and South India, made out of roasted semolina or rice flour
70. Vada pav: Fried potato wrapped in a bun (a popular snack in Maharashtra)
71. Vangi bhaji: A curry made out of brinjal
72. Wada: Traditional mansion, usually found in Maharashtra
73. Warli: A style of art associated with the tribal communities and popular in the Northern parts of Maharashtra
74. *Fursungicha Faster Fene*: Faster Fene of Fursungi
75. B. R. Bhagwat (1910-2001): Eminent children's writer of Maharashtra
76. Rujuta Diwekar: India's leading nutrition and exercise science expert

# Useful Resources

For further reading about Usher syndrome as well as adoption in India, here are some useful online and offline resources.

**Usher Syndrome**

1. Usher Syndrome Coalition: www.usher-syndrome.org
2. NoisyVision Onlus: www.noisyvision.org
3. Organisation for Rare Diseases India: www.ordindia.in
4. Visual Bucket List Foundation: www.thevisualbucketlistfoundation.com
5. Beth David Institute, Tel Aviv, Israel: www.cdb.org.il/en/about-us

**Adoption in India**

1. Bharatiya Samaj Seva Kendra: www.facebook.com/BharatiyaSamajSevaKendra
2. Atmaja - Association of Adoptive Parents: www.atmaja.org.in

3. Sudatta Adoption Parivar: www.sudatta.org
4. Central Adoption Resource Authority: www.cara.nic.in
5. Indian Association for Promotion of Adoption and Child Welfare: www.iapacw.org

# Places Mentioned in the Book

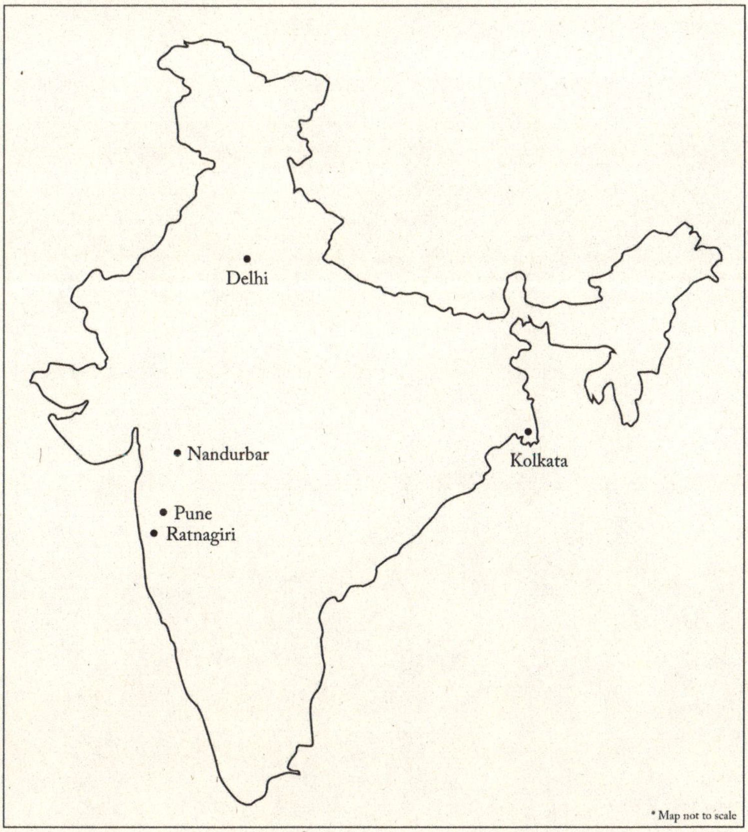

# About the Illustrator

After twenty plus years in advertising, **Niloufer Wadia** quit her job to follow her passion—illustration and fine art painting. In 2015, a lucky break in an online competition by Pratham Books gave Niloufer her first children's picture book. Since then, picture books and chapter books fill the largest chunk of her illustration assignments.

She has illustrated over twenty-five picture and chapter books for a wide selection of publishers and several illustrated covers too along with a few for adult novels too. The publishers she has worked with include Pratham

Books, Karadi Tales, Tulika Publishers, Scholastic India, Random House New York, Amazon Westland, Amazon Red Panda, Bloomsbury, Duckbill Publishers, and Hay House India. To see her illustrations, check out her Instagram profile: @niloufer.artist.

# About the Author

**Vikas Prakash Joshi** is a writer by nature and nurture and not by compulsion, ambition, or conscious choice. His writing career started in school at the age of eleven when his contributions were published in the school newspaper and magazines, and he won prizes in intra-class competitions and intra-school contests. He wrote over 150 letters to prominent English newspapers in India at an early age, winning six 'Letter of the Week' contests in leading newspapers and magazines before becoming a newspaper columnist in *Junior Herald* at the age of eighteen. His columns and short stories in

*Junior Herald* reached tens of thousands of readers, and his articles were published in national-level newspapers and in well-known youth magazines in the USA like *Skipping Stones* and *Teen Ink*. He subsequently won awards in writing essay contests in city, state, national, and international levels. One of his essays, 'The World's Youngest Democracy', was a first prize winner in a global essay competition organised by the Centre for International Private Enterprise in 2013, beating out entries from 66 countries.

He has done a BA in English literature from the Pune-based Symbiosis College of Arts and Commerce, a postgraduate diploma in journalism from the Asian College of Journalism, Chennai (where he received the prestigious South Asia Foundation Madanjeet Singh Scholarship), and an MA in development studies from the Tata Institute of Social Sciences, Mumbai. He has travelled and written for leading Indian publications like *The Caravan, Hindustan Times, The Wire, The Hindu, DNA, Sakal Times* and reported from diverse parts of India including Maharashtra, Punjab, Karnataka, Tamil Nadu, Gujarat, and Odisha. His essays, articles, and short stories have been translated and published in thirty-one languages, both Indian and foreign, and in twenty-three countries. His stories have also been published in two anthologies: *Inspired by Tagore* (British Council) and *Fables* (Cognition Tree). He has also set up and hosted Pune's first and only podcast on writing and literature, *Literary Gupshup*.

Besides writing, he has won nine awards in club-level public speaking contests organized by Toastmasters International, where he holds an advanced communicator silver (ACS) in public speaking. He has been a freelance model for a fashion photographer Ajinkya Jadhav and for Kalam Kaushal, a Jaipur based clothing store. His hobbies include public speaking, cooking, travelling, and reading. He is currently based in Pune where he lives with his family.

*My Name Is Cinnamon* is his first book.

Joshi.vikas500@gmail.com

@Authorvikasprakashjoshi

@Vikas-prakash-joshi

@AuthorVikasPrakashJoshi

HAY HOUSE

CONNECT WITH

# HAY HOUSE

ONLINE

hayhouse.co.in

@hayhouseindia

@hayhouseindia

@hayhouseindia

Join the conversation about latest products, events, exclusive offers, contests, giveaways and more.

*'The gateways to wisdom and knowledge are always open.'*

**Louise Hay**